Sara always got her man. This time would be no different.

Her gut instinct told her that something in what she'd just seen and heard presented a key piece of evidence in her current investigative puzzle.

She flipped open her phone and pressed a series of keys, transmitting photo after photo to the Prescott Personal Securities offices for identification.

Sara might be about to morph into the perfect picture of a Denver socialite, but there wasn't any reason why she couldn't launch some additional investigative work into action behind the scenes while she made nice with Kyle Prescott.

And nice was exactly what she intended to make.

For now.

W9-DJQ-381

KATHLEEN LONG

HIGH SOCIETY SABOTAGE

TORONTO • NEW YORK • LONDON
AMSTERDAM • PARIS • SYDNEY • HAMBURG
STOCKHOLM • ATHENS • TOKYO • MILAN • MADRID
PRAGUE • WARSAW • BUDAPEST • AUCKLAND

Special thanks and acknowledgment are given to Kathleen Long for her contribution to the BODYGUARDS UNLIMITED, DENVER, COLORADO miniseries.

For Denise Zaza and Allison Lyons, with gratitude.

ISBN-13: 978-0-373-69260-6
ISBN-10:   0-373-69260-9

HIGH SOCIETY SABOTAGE

ABOUT THE AUTHOR

After a career spent spinning words for clients ranging from corporate CEOs to talking fruits and vegetables, Kathleen now finds great joy spinning a world of fictional characters, places and plots. Having decided to pursue her writing goals when her first daughter taught her that life is short and dreams are for chasing, Kathleen is now an award-winning author of breathtaking romantic suspense for the Harlequin Intrigue line.

A RIO Award of Excellence winner and a National Readers Choice, Booksellers Best and Holt Medallion nominee, her greatest reward can be found in the letters and e-mails she receives from her readers. Nothing makes her happier than knowing one of her stories has provided a few hours of escape and enjoyment, offering a chance to forget about life for a little while.

Along with her husband, infant daughter and one very neurotic sheltie, Kathleen divides her time between suburban Philadelphia and the New Jersey seashore, where she can often be found hands on keyboard— bare toes in sand—spinning tales. After all, life doesn't get much better than that.

Please visit her at www.kathleenlong.com or drop her a line at P.O. Box 3864, Cherry Hill, NJ 08034.

Books by Kathleen Long

HARLEQUIN INTRIGUE

CAST OF CHARACTERS

Sara Montgomery—An investigator for Prescott Personal Securities, she's gone undercover as a debutante to expose the hidden conspiracy at TCM.

Kyle Prescott—An executive at media conglomerate TCM, someone's forged his signature on a series of land deals in the Denver area. Will Kyle take the ultimate blame?

Stephen Turner—The CEO of TCM and stepfather to Kyle Prescott, his company's reputation is on the line.

Peter Turner—Stephen's son and Kyle's half brother, Peter has never measured up to Kyle's reputation or charm. What is he capable of doing in order to make his own mark?

Dwayne Johnson—Kyle Prescott's second-in-command at TCM, he's the only person authorized to use his boss's signature. Did he purposefully commit fraud? Or is he an innocent pawn?

Buddy Forman—Head of security at TCM, he's determined to keep things in order. But how committed is he to company security?

Evangeline Prescott—Head of Prescott Personal Securities, she's determined to bring the guilty party to justice even if that person is her stepson, Kyle.

Chapter One

Ten minutes into the party, Sara Montgomery knew she'd been spotted by a potential target. And she couldn't be more pleased.

She stole a glance at Kyle Prescott as he worked the large birthday party for his stepfather. He wound his way through the society and corporate types gathered at the Turner ranch as if he'd done so all his life.

Sara laughed softly to herself. He *had* done so all his life.

She noted the sideways glance he sent her way. One corner of his mouth lifted, as if he knew she watched him.

She smiled, hoping the man would read her expression as a sign of interest and not for what it really was—a smile of satisfaction. Satisfaction that she'd found a potential means to infiltrate TCM, her latest assignment for Prescott Personal Securities and the true reason Sara found herself at TCM CEO Stephen Turner's birthday party.

After being briefed on the investigative findings to date, Sara had developed several options for achieving her goal. Oddly enough, charming her way into Kyle Prescott's life had fallen somewhere toward the bottom of the list.

As the man mingled with other partygoers, circling ever closer to where she chatted with a TCM employee, Sara realized she should have put Kyle Prescott at the top of her list.

He was the perfect in, assuming she played her cards right. Which she would.

The playboy represented everything she loathed about the society scene, but what did it matter?

Sara had a job to do, and she'd do it well. She always did. She wasn't about to let the sour taste left in her mouth by a polite society gathering such as this one distract her from her objective.

Access enough inside information on TCM to find out who was operating the bogus Kingston Trust and the scheme to buy up land for the oil beneath—no matter what the ultimate cost.

Considering the rising body count of Kingston Trust investors, Sara knew she had to work quickly, and effectively.

If Kyle Prescott represented the pawn she needed to get inside the workings of TCM, so be it.

She had every intention of stopping the conspiracy before the next victim fell.

The mission called for her to blend in with the society crowd, so blend in she would.

She took a sip of her champagne, noting the weight of the crystal flute in her hand. The ballroom at the Turner ranch had been decked out from corner to corner in only the finest linens, flowers and crystal.

Candles, which Sara understood to be hand-dipped by children at a local charity Stephen Turner supported, adorned each table as centerpieces.

While the glitz and glamour of the entire scene made the small hairs at the base of Sara's neck lift, the presence of the candles provided a tender, human touch that made the entire visual tolerable.

While Sara had always hated the party scene, her older sister, Annemarie, had lived for it. She'd died for it, as well, being murdered at a party days before what would have been her coming-out ceremony.

Sara had refused to attend the same party and her parents had never forgiven her, as if somehow Annemarie's death wouldn't have happened had Sara been in attendance.

Sara's heart gave a sharp twist, the familiar ache squeezing her chest. Maybe they were right. Maybe she could have made a difference, had she only been there for Annemarie.

Sara had gone through with her own debut a year after they buried Annemarie—part of the Montgomery family plan to prove the unsolved murder of their oldest daughter hadn't destroyed them.

Attending the debutantes' ball was the last thing Sara ever did to please her parents. They certainly didn't approve of the life she'd created for herself since then.

She blinked away the memories as Kyle Prescott neared. Now was the time for razor-sharp focus on the present, not blurry-edged memories of the past.

She studied the man casually, yet carefully, as the TCM employee by her side blathered on and on about global marketing.

Sara didn't feel guilty about partially tuning out the man's words. She was more than capable of listening closely enough to respond when necessary, but she'd already determined his position in the company could lend nothing to her investigation.

She had no problem being blunt and, truth was, she had no use for him.

Kyle Prescott, on the other hand, was an entirely different story.

As head of TCM's international rights division and stepson to Stephen Turner, he was no doubt privy to key corporate information and accounting.

Perfect. Just the foot in the door Sara needed.

Kyle Prescott kept his distance from where Sara stood, chatting and shaking hands with those gathered, but she felt his focus on her. Felt his gaze on her.

She'd always had a sixth sense about being watched, and that sixth sense was working overtime right now.

She glanced down at her dress. A dress she would

have never voluntarily chosen, but one that was obviously having the intended effect now that she'd set her sights on Kyle.

While the other women present dripped diamonds and sequins, Sara had chosen a classic, yet seductive, red, silk dress. The sleeveless style showed off her lean shoulders, while the surplice front revealed just enough skin to hint at the curves that hid beneath.

She'd pulled her one piece of real jewelry out of its storage spot in the bottom of her jewelry box. The diamond choker encircled her neck, small star-shaped pendants dangling toward her cleavage.

The skirt of the dress stopped precisely at her knees, revealing nothing but the long expanse of her bare legs, supported by her sexiest pair of three-inch heels.

Kyle began to make his move, and Sara adjusted her stance, working to send the signal she waited for his approach. He shifted his course through the crowd, casually moving straight for her.

His black hair shone in the room's subtle lighting, his blue eyes so light they glowed like beacons from the handsome lines of his suntanned face. A day's worth of stubble lined his jaw and Sara wondered how hard he had to work at maintaining the slightly unkempt look.

His manner of dress, however, had nothing unkempt about it.

The man's black tux fit as though it had been tailored just for his broad-shouldered build, and she had no doubt it had been. The expensive material hung flawlessly on him as he moved toward her, the white collar in sharp contrast to both his suntanned face and the tux itself.

He moved confidently, securely, proudly owning every inch of his well-built six-foot frame. It was there that she saw the resemblance to his late father. Robert Prescott had moved with the same self-assuredness.

She knew from her preparation for this assignment that Kyle was only a few years younger than she, but as far as Sara was concerned, they were a lifetime of differences apart from one another.

His had been a life of luxury and pampering. Hers had not. A choice she'd made. A choice her family had never forgiven her for.

But Kyle Prescott?

Kyle Prescott was a man used to getting his way, even at the tender age of twenty-eight.

He strode toward her now, his gaze riveted to hers. She stood her ground, not faltering in the least. She didn't rattle easily—never had.

She stiffened, resenting the man before he so much as made his first move, before he delivered his first line. And that first line was on its way. No doubt about it.

Sara was about to experience the legendary Kyle Prescott charm firsthand.

She could hardly wait.

KYLE HAD SPOTTED the petite but leggy brunette the instant she walked from the valet area toward the party. He'd been dreading his stepfather's birthday party, having never felt much more than obligation toward the man, but perhaps things were looking up.

He'd hoped to speak to his second in command at International, Dwayne Johnson, but the man had been a no-show. Big surprise there.

Kyle had left a none-too-kind voice mail about the call he'd received from a TCM investor in reference to a disturbing memo bearing Kyle's signature. A signature he had no recollection of writing.

Kyle might be fairly apathetic when it came to the day-to-day business of TCM, but he'd be damned if he'd let someone get away with transacting any sort of business under his name, at least not without him having final approval.

He laughed to himself.

Johnson had probably been so surprised by not only the voice mail, but also the fact Kyle had checked his messages, that he'd dropped on the spot.

No matter.

He'd catch up to him later.

For now, Kyle had a fresh target in mind.

He watched as the woman shook hands with another guest then engaged in what appeared to be comfortable small talk.

Her red dress hugged all the right curves and left a little more to the imagination than he'd like, but perhaps that was what turned his head. She had plenty of sex appeal, but didn't flaunt her attributes like most of the other women at the party.

Kyle continued his casual conversation, all the while keeping one eye on the brunette, doing his best not to stare at the way her brown hair shone under the light from the chandeliers. Several loose tendrils had found their way out of her hairdo and brushed softly against her neck whenever she laughed or tipped her head.

Breathtaking. The woman was absolutely breathtaking. The expanse of bare leg between the hem of her skirt and her barely there sandals didn't hurt, either.

He smiled.

Since he couldn't seem to shake the playboy reputation that preceded him wherever he went, he might as well live up to it.

No time like the present to start.

He closed the space between them and extended his hand, enjoying the feel of her soft yet sure touch as she slid her hand inside his.

"Come here often?" he asked, a smile teasing the corners of his lips as he gave her hand one quick pump then held on tight.

The woman tipped her head sideways, exposing the length of her slender neck. "Does that line actually ever work for you?" Her eyebrows lifted coyly.

Kyle did nothing to contain his laughter. He had

no idea who the beauty before him was, but he had every intention of finding out.

Her light green eyes sparked like those of a filly begging to be tamed, and her dark, wavy hair dared him to undo her twist and run his fingers through the thick strands.

"Why, yes, ma'am. It typically works like a charm."

He glared at the TCM employee by the woman's side and the man slinked away, effectively dismissed with just one glance.

Kyle continued to hold the woman's hand, taking careful note of the way the front of the wrapped dress gaped under the strain of her outstretched arm.

"Kyle Prescott." He gave her hand another gentle pump, then released his grip.

"Sara Montgomery." She met his gaze unflinchingly. Kyle spotted her strong will instantly.

He'd bedded many a beauty in his days, yet there was something in this woman's eyes the others had lacked. A light he'd never seen before. A focus.

A challenge?

Lord knew he could use some excitement in his life. Maybe Ms. Montgomery would be just the thing to occupy his days—and nights—for a spell.

"How do you know my stepfather?"

"Family acquaintance." He watched as Sara gave a dismissive wave of her hand. "Tough work, isn't it?

One function after another. Fund-raisers. Birthday parties. Black-tie auctions."

She visibly caught herself, as if her comments might be offensive.

He grinned.

"I didn't mean this particular birthday party." She let out a small sigh. "Just the circuit in general."

Kyle found himself mesmerized by the twinkle in her eyes. "I wouldn't know."

She narrowed her gaze. "Your reputation precedes you, Mr. Prescott. I'm sure you're at one party or another every night of the week."

Before Kyle could answer, his half brother Peter stepped between them, extending his hand toward Sara.

She took a step back, startled by the sudden movement.

"Peter Turner."

"Sara Montgomery."

Kyle bit back an unusual wave of jealousy. Let Peter find his own companion for the evening. Ms. Montgomery was obviously miles out of his league.

"You're as beautiful as your sister was."

An emotion Kyle couldn't quite put his finger on passed across Sara's features.

"You knew her?" she asked.

"I was a great admirer." Peter nodded. "She was the one person who took the time to talk to me when I was a kid. I remember her from some of the parties Mother and Father took me to."

His expression turned grim. "I was very young, but I still remember the shock of hearing she'd been murdered."

Montgomery.

Kyle knew the last name had rung a bell.

He watched as Peter pinned Sara with a look that fell far short of sympathy. "I would imagine her death ripped your family apart?"

Enough.

Kyle stepped between Peter and Sara, glaring at his half brother. "Leave it to you to turn the conversation to tragedy, especially on an evening as gorgeous as this one." He turned to Sara. "My apologies."

But before she could answer, loud voices sounded from the far side of the gathering.

His mother stood, hands on hips, hot anger flaring in her cheeks and eyes, as she screamed at the caterer.

"Only an imbecile would serve on these dishes." Olivia Turner gestured wildly then tossed a plate against the parquet floor. The sound of china shattering was unmistakable.

"An imbecile!" she continued ranting. "If you think you're getting your final payment, you've got another thing coming."

Kyle's stepfather stood at her side, fingers wrapped around her elbow, obviously trying to calm her and move her away from where she and the caterer stood over what appeared to be several shattered dishes.

"Unhand me." Olivia spun on her husband as the shocked partygoers fell silent, watching her every move. "Don't you dare try to placate me after this man's—" she pointed accusingly at the caterer "—outrageous behavior."

"Excuse me," Peter said softly. "It seems Mother could use a drink."

SARA'S MIND WHIRLED with possibilities as Stephen Turner succeeded in moving his wife away from the tables of food. The poor caterer worked feverishly to clean up all evidence of Olivia's tirade.

Perhaps the woman had been justified in her actions, but surely a public display such as the one she'd just caused fell somewhere outside the acceptable parameters of polite society.

Sara had heard rumors about Olivia Turner's tendency toward odd behavior. She'd just witnessed proof of those allegations firsthand.

"I apologize for my brother's rudeness." The rumble of Kyle Prescott's voice cut through Sara's thoughts.

She shifted her focus to his face, noting the lines of stress that had appeared following his mother's outburst.

Annemarie. Her thoughts turned back to the awkward conversation with Kyle's half brother.

"He took me by surprise," Sara answered. She waved one hand as if she weren't bothered by Peter's comment, when the truth was she'd been blindsided.

Peter Turner's sudden remarks had left her feeling raw and exposed.

The orchestra swung into a slow, melodic tune and Kyle held out his hand. "Dance?"

Sara slipped her fingers into his. "It would be my pleasure."

They moved to the center of the dance floor, other partygoers moving out of their way as if they were the Red Sea parting for the prodigal son.

For a split second, nerves fluttered to life in Sara's stomach but she willed them away.

Now wasn't the time to feel out of her element. Now was the time to revel in her surroundings.

She swayed to the music, following Kyle's obviously practiced lead as the orchestra played on. The heat of Kyle's fingers burned through the thin material of her dress at the small of her back, but she held her composure. Held her cover.

"I don't remember seeing you at all these awful society events you mentioned." Kyle's lips quirked into a grin. "Are you sure you aren't just crashing this party?"

If he only knew.

Sara graced him with her warmest smile, gazing up into his deep blue eyes. "Let's just say I've been off the circuit for a bit." Not a complete lie. "But I'm back now."

His grin widened and he pulled her closer. "Lucky for me."

Sara shifted to slide her fingers higher on Kyle's shoulder. "That remains to be seen, doesn't it?"

When the music stopped, Kyle moved toward the edge of the dance floor, never letting go of Sara's hand. She concentrated on remaining upright in the ridiculous heels she'd purchased just for this occasion.

If she were smart, she'd have practiced walking in the contraptions before tonight.

When they reached the far side of the ballroom, Kyle spun on her, daring her with his expression. "I could use a change of scenery." One dark brow lifted. "Do you ride?"

Sara glanced down at her heels. "I do but I don't think there's a horse anywhere that would appreciate these shoes."

A smile spread wide across Kyle's face, the tension that had been there before their dance completely gone now.

"Not horses."

Still holding her hand, he led her through the crowd and out into the cool, night air. He tipped his chin toward one of the guesthouses where a Harley gleamed under a floodlight. "Ever ridden a beauty like that one?"

Sara narrowed her gaze. "What do you think? That I get driven everywhere, Mr. Prescott?"

One dark brow crooked, amusement shimmering in his gaze. "If the shoe fits. And, please, call me Kyle."

"For your information, I've ridden plenty of bikes." She bluffed completely.

She'd been on the back of a motorcycle once, and it came nowhere close to the size of the giant Kyle had pointed out.

He crossed his arms over his chest and grinned, the move lighting up his features. "Then perhaps you'd like to prove yourself."

She inwardly cursed the traitorous tumble her stomach took in response to his smile.

"Now?" she asked.

Sara's plan was working beautifully. If Kyle Prescott was ready to whisk her away on one of his infamous Harley rides through the mountains, she'd made more progress today than she'd hoped for.

He nodded in answer to her question, daring her with his pale eyes. "You game?"

She read the unspoken question buried in his words and suggestively traced a finger down her throat to the hollow at the base of her neck. She ran her finger over her choker. Back and forth. Back and forth.

"I'm always game, Mr. Prescott…Kyle." She corrected herself.

When he offered his arm, Sara slipped her hand inside, taking note of his well-muscled upper arm and the lean body against which he tightly pressed her hand. She gave herself a mental nod of congratulations.

Was she game?

Most definitely.

She was always game to get her man. And Kyle Prescott promised to be a worthy—and challenging—opponent.

Chapter Two

Kyle handled the bike effortlessly, as if he spent much of his time roaming the vast mountain roads outside of Denver. Sara smiled to herself as she followed his lead, leaning into the curve as they rounded a bend.

From what she knew about Kyle Prescott, his days were supposed to be spent running the international rights division of TCM, but rumor had it he practiced a more absent management style. He rarely showed up at the office, and when he did, he remained isolated in his office. Nothing more.

That particular description of him didn't jibe with the outgoing, charming man she'd met tonight. One of the personas was an act. All she had to do was figure out which one it was.

Sara tightened her grip around Kyle's waist, pressing her body tightly against his back. What the heck. If she were going to play the role of a blinded-by-money-and-charm Kyle Prescott groupie, she might as well go all out.

She let her mind wander momentarily, taking in the breathtaking scenery illuminated by the full moon. Majestic slabs of red rock gave way to deep valleys dropping far below the roadside. Summer wildflowers smattered the mountainside with what would surely be vivid splashes of color in the light of day.

For the slightest moment she wanted to tell Kyle to stop—wanted to take just a minute out of the investigation to enjoy the beauty before her.

How long had it been since she'd been up here? *Too long.*

She and her sister used to sneak up this road all the time once Annemarie had gotten her license, but Sara had devoted the years since Annemarie's death to taking down criminals, not sightseeing.

She'd loved her time in the FBI, but being part of the Prescott Personal Securities team was a dream come true. Her undercover assignment to investigate the media conglomerate TCM was something she could sink her teeth into, and her first chance to truly shine as part of PPS.

She could only hope Annemarie would be proud. Sara might not have been able to solve her sister's murder, but she'd solved others. She'd eased other families' pain. Try as she might to content herself with that fact, it somehow was never enough.

Kyle eased the bike to the side of the road, snapping Sara's focus back to the man—and the case— at hand. He cut the bike's engine, climbed off the massive machine then helped Sara down from the back of the seat, no easy feat in her heels and dress.

When he kept her fingers tightly in his grip, she resisted the urge to pull them free, instead playing the part of the smitten female.

She followed him to the lookout's edge, gazing down into a valley of jagged rock, stands of evergreens and lush green rolling hillsides. If she weren't mistaken, the Turner ranch lay in the distance. She could just make out the shape of the buildings and the well-lit grounds.

"Isn't that—?"

"Sure is," Kyle answered before she finished her sentence.

He dropped her hand, leaving her fingers oddly cool where his had been. Sara shook off the unwanted sensation, silently reminding herself not to be pulled under by the man's obviously practiced charm.

When he stepped behind her and placed his hands on her shoulders, she fought the urge to toss him over one shoulder and onto his back. Her automatic self-defense response screamed at her to make the move, but her undercover role demanded she stay put.

"Look at this land." His breath brushed past her ear and a shiver of awareness traced its way across Sara's shoulders. "This is my favorite place to visit."

And probably with a different female each time, Sara thought.

"Gorgeous," she answered. "I can't imagine why anyone would want to develop an inch of these hills."

"Well, within limits, some development can actually add to the local tax base."

His quick response took her by surprise, not at all what she'd expected.

"Matter of fact," he continued, "some might look at it as a win-win. Additional housing, additional tax dollars, some pocket change for the developer, and you just never know. There might be oil in those hills."

Oil.

Land held by at least three of the dead investors' companies was known oil land. Maybe Kyle Prescott represented even more than the perfect means to infiltrate TCM. Maybe he also represented the perfect means to infiltrate the investing scheme.

Sara spun on him, seizing the opportunity to push for information. "You can't be serious."

His vivid gaze widened with evident surprise. Apparently Kyle Prescott wasn't used to receiving criticism from his romantic conquests.

He frowned slightly. "I'm completely serious."

Sara gestured to the expanse below them. "You actually think losing a portion of this land is a good thing?"

He narrowed his eyes and nodded. "Progress is progress, babe."

Babe.

She spun back toward the view before he could

spot the hot color firing in her cheeks. All it would take would be one swift kick to send the man flying off the cliff and into the valley he was apparently so anxious to see developed.

TCM, Sara reminded herself. Stay focused on TCM.

But she couldn't quite ignore Kyle Prescott's know-it-all arrogance. She waited until her face cooled, then shifted her gaze back in his direction. He stood staring past her, at the Turner ranch, if she weren't mistaken.

"What about land preservation?" she asked.

His focus snapped from the view to her face. "What about it?"

The intensity of his focus rattled her ever so slightly. She didn't like the sensation—didn't like it at all. She forced her thoughts back to their conversation.

If she could keep him talking about land and oil, he might let some useful information slip into their conversation.

"I'd think you'd be more concerned about international deals than about land acquisitions." She gave an innocent shrug, working to maintain an air of innocence. "Isn't that your area of expertise?"

He studied her for a long moment then leaned close. "Is there a reason you're so concerned about the land, Ms. Montgomery? I assure you I have far more interesting areas of expertise."

Sara arched one brow. "Can't a girl care about her environment?"

A sly grin slid across Kyle's lips. "Sweetheart, you can care about whatever you want."

The man's arrogant tone sent anger flicking to life in Sara's gut. Heat rose from her neck to her face. This time, she made no move to hide her reaction.

"I'm always amazed when a man of your obvious wealth and social status won't use that power for good."

"When good playboys go bad." He leaned even closer. Too close.

Sara held her ground, squinting at him. Their conversation was getting her nowhere. He had yet to give her a straight answer. The man was hiding something, and she had every intention of finding out what.

"Mr. Prescott—"

"I could have sworn I told you to call me Kyle."

He made his move quickly, as if he'd made it countless times before, leaning into Sara and cupping her face in the palm of one hand.

When he closed his mouth over hers, she opened her lips to protest, only to find his lips matching her moves, his tongue tangling with hers, exploring, tasting.

Traitorous heat ignited deep inside her and Sara wound her hands around his neck and into his slightly too long hair, noting the silky texture and wondering how much money he spent on salon treatments.

When he splayed his palms fully on the small of

her back and pulled her body tight against his, her only thought was of how good he felt.

The hard expanse of his chest.

The warmth of his body against hers.

His obvious arousal pressed against her stomach.

Sara blinked herself back into reality before she lost control of the situation, breaking away from his kiss and pushing him out to arm's length.

Kyle didn't release his grip, however. Instead he gave her waist a squeeze and turned on his mega-watt smile.

Sara had to admit he was good. *Very good.*

She could see why woman after woman fell for him, only to be discarded when he'd grown bored or received a more enticing offer.

Well, if she'd learned one thing over the years it was that the more you pushed a guy like Kyle away, the more he'd come begging. She decided then and there on her plan of attack. As much as she hated playing games, a round of hard-to-get seemed to be in order.

She drew in a dramatic breath and splayed her hand across her neck. "I think it best we get back to the ranch."

Without saying a word, Kyle let his gaze drift from her mouth, to her hand, over the swell of her breasts, along the lines of her skirt, down the length of her legs, then slowly back up until he met her eyes.

The seconds passed in slow motion, each moment pure torture as her body heated beneath his gaze.

She swallowed just before his eyes met hers.

"You'd better wear this." He shrugged out of his tux jacket then draped it around her shoulders. "You wouldn't want to catch a chill."

Oh, he was *good.*

But she could be even better.

KYLE MENTALLY BERATED himself as he maneuvered the bike along the mountain road down from the lookout. When he got a bit too close to the shoulder, he tried to snap himself back into focus by shoving Sara Montgomery out of his head, but it didn't work.

The heat of her arms pressed around his body and the memory of their kiss lingered on his lips. He'd kissed a lot of women in his day, no doubt about it, but no kiss had ever been quite like this one. It wasn't that her pulling away had made it different. *She* had made it different. Plain and simple.

Sara Montgomery ignited a sensation inside him that had never been ignited. She intrigued him. Genuinely intrigued him.

She shifted against him as he pulled into a straight patch of road. Her soft curves pressed into his back, and if he didn't know better, he'd swear the woman was trying to torture him.

His body remained in a heightened state of awareness even now, at least fifteen minutes since their kiss.

He ran their discussion through his head for the umpteenth time. The truth of the matter was he agreed with everything she said.

He hated to see the sprawl that crept into the land at the base of the mountains. If he had his way, no one would ever be able to develop here again.

Kyle couldn't quite put his finger on why he'd lied in order to get Sara's response. Maybe he'd done it to get a rise out of her, or to measure her response.

He'd been pleasantly surprised when she hadn't agreed with him, as most of the upper crust in the region would have.

Land equaled power in these parts and oil was the Holy Grail. The more land you owned, the better chance you had of striking it rich. He should know. He'd watched several local power brokers find success after success in recent months with lucky land buyouts.

The voice mail he'd received planted itself front and center on his radar screen again. Was that what the man had been referring to? Had he been accusing Kyle of taking part in some sort of investment scheme? If so, the man couldn't be further off base.

Kyle hadn't taken part, out of his love for the area's wilderness, but he had to admit the money was enough to tempt many an environmentalist to the dark side. He, however, wasn't one of them.

He shouldn't have let Sara go on as he did without telling her the truth, but it had been a pleasure to see her passion when she spoke, her determination when she explained her stance.

The woman was refreshing, a treat he intended to sample fully when she offered. And she would in time. They always did.

If she thought the hard-to-get act was original, she needed to think again. That particular tactic was tired as well as ineffectual, at least where Kyle was concerned.

He'd been surprised she hadn't broken away from their kiss more quickly, but the biggest question bouncing around his brain was why she'd agreed to the ride in the first place.

The action didn't match the coolness she'd otherwise shown. He wondered what she was after. His money? His connections? History showed it would be one or the other. It always was.

Before he could give the topic another thought, Sara leaned forward and tried to yell something to him. The noise of the bike's engine and the thickness of the helmet he wore muffled her voice.

He shook his head to let her know he hadn't made out a word she'd said. He dropped a look to his rearview mirror just as she extricated one arm from around his waist and leaned forward, jerking her thumb toward the road behind them.

Kyle knew what she was referring to as soon as she made the gesture. He was already studying the approaching headlights in the mirror.

The vehicle appeared to be an SUV. Dark. Sleek. Heavily tinted windows.

Not your average drive-in-the-mountains fare.

The SUV moved dangerously close to the rear tire of the bike and Kyle accelerated, adrenaline surging to life inside him.

Was the guy behind him nuts? Or was he challenging him to a little road race?

The SUV pulled into the oncoming lane as they approached the next hairpin turn.

What in the—?

Kyle maneuvered away from the too-close black vehicle, yet still maintained control of the bike.

"Hold on," he yelled into the mountain air, knowing Sara most likely couldn't hear a thing.

Her arms tightened around his waist, bolstering his resolve to get them away from the maniac in the SUV.

They cleared the curve, but the SUV swerved toward them in the straightaway, pushing Kyle and Sara dangerously close to the edge of the cliff.

Kyle gritted his teeth, determined not to lose control. His father had been killed in an accident and Kyle had no intention of carrying on the family tradition.

The next hairpin turn approached. Kyle knew they wouldn't make it. They'd have to ditch, but how would he be able to warn Sara?

The SUV swung toward them, brushing mere inches from their legs. Sara screamed something, but Kyle couldn't make it out.

Damn it. It would be bad enough if he were alone on the bike, but with Sara on the back, he was responsible for saving not just himself, but also the beautiful stranger.

The SUV swerved again, and the front tire of the motorcycle nipped into the rocks and dirt along the edge of the cliff. They faltered, and the bike bobbled from side to side.

The SUV accelerated out around the next curve and out of sight, as if the driver knew what was about to happen, knew he'd succeeded in his dangerous game.

Kyle did his best to slow the motorcycle without losing complete control, but it was too late.

The tires went out from under the bike and they were sliding, dirt and gravel flying, obscuring his view. They slid, and pain exploded through Kyle as the weight of the bike did its damage. Sara's arms suddenly were no longer around his waist and fear ripped through him.

Had she gone over the cliff? Had she been injured—or worse—because of him?

That was the question haunting Kyle as the mountain fell away beneath him and he and his Harley went over the edge.

Chapter Three

Sara spit the dirt out of her mouth and reached for the strap of her helmet even as she launched herself into action.

She'd been able to jump from the motorcycle as they wrecked, but Kyle hadn't been so lucky. She'd tried to tell him to jump, but he'd no doubt been unable to hear her above the noise of the motorcycle's engine.

He and the bike were nowhere to be seen. When Sara spotted a telltale gash in the earth at the edge of the road, bile clawed its way up her throat.

It would take a miracle to survive a fall over the cliff.

She scrambled toward the edge of the roadway, ignoring the pain in every muscle in her body. She held her breath as she peered over the edge, utter amazement ripping through her at the sight of Kyle sprawled on a section of rock just below her. The bike, however, was nowhere to be found.

"Kyle!"

Sara yelled his name when she spotted movement in his arms and legs. To her amazement, he pulled himself into a sitting position, each move an obvious struggle.

"You're all right?" He spat out the words as he tipped his face toward her, pulling off his helmet as he did so.

The arrogance so prevalent in his expression just minutes earlier was gone. Instead, he searched her face, sincere concern plastered across his features.

Sara nodded, surprised by the absence of any hint of self-awareness on his part.

"Are you hurt badly?" she asked.

He shook his head. "I'll live."

She dropped onto her belly, reaching for him. "Give me your hands."

Kyle gave her one hand while he used the other to pull himself up the jagged face of the section of mountain.

Sara pulled with all her might, being careful to let him set the pace. When he cleared the top, he dropped onto his side, wincing in pain. His shirt had been ripped and blood seeped through the white fabric in several spots.

She reached for him, but caught herself at the last moment, deciding against the move. "We have to get you help."

He shook his head, the muscles in his jaw tensing. "We have to get back. Get you checked out."

"I'm all right. A bit battered, but nothing's broken."

He gave his head another shake. "We still need to get you cleaned up."

Sara glanced up and down the road. They'd encountered no other vehicle during their trip except the SUV. "Any ideas?"

Kyle pulled off his boot and reached inside, pressing something along the seam.

"What are you doing?"

He lifted his pale gaze to hers and gave her a weak smile. "Automatic tracking signal."

"You have got to be kidding me." She shook her head, letting a laugh of relief slide between her lips.

He shot her a wink. "Never underestimate the power of technology."

KYLE LEANED into the stream of steaming water pouring from the showerhead, his palms splayed against the cool tile. He'd been lucky. Bumped and bruised and he'd no doubt feel much worse in the morning, but he'd survived. That was a whole lot more than he could say for his bike.

He'd dropped Sara at her home and sent her car over with one of TCM's drivers. His personal physician had followed close behind.

Dr. Franklin had checked in a short while ago to let Kyle know Ms. Montgomery would be just fine.

Kyle winced as the water stung his still raw wounds. He couldn't believe how close they'd both come to dying.

Who had been behind the wheel of the SUV? And had the driver's actions been done out of sport, or out of malice? If malice, who was the target? Surely not Sara. They must have been after him, but why?

He hadn't planned to go up into the mountains, so if the attack had been made purposefully, he and Sara had been followed from the time they'd left the party. No one but the two of them knew where they had been headed.

Kyle thought of the alleged memo bearing his signature and the call he'd placed to Dwayne. Surely today's accident had nothing to do with his demand for an explanation, did it?

He shook his head.

Pure coincidence. Though, he'd never been a fan of coincidence.

He twisted off the water and reached for a towel. After he'd dabbed at his wounds and anchored the towel snuggly around his waist, he padded barefoot to his personal office.

Here, he could access the TCM computers twenty-four hours a day. No one knew of his setup, not even his stepfather.

The one perk of his bad-boy reputation was the fact that everyone had forgotten he actually had a brain beneath his well-styled hair.

He stopped as he passed through the kitchen to snag a tall, cold beer from the fridge. He deserved a drink—or several—after today's events.

Kyle popped the cap and took a long pull. Even though he'd literally fallen off a cliff and had had one of the worst days of his life, he couldn't avoid the way he'd felt since the moment he first met Sara Montgomery.

Shaking her hand.

Debating land issues.

The feel of her slender shoulders beneath his touch.

His stomach tightened and he chastised himself as he dropped into his leather desk chair. He'd never let a woman get to him before, so what made this one different?

For one, she didn't hesitate to argue with him.

He smiled. Now there was something new.

Typically, the women he met were so eager to please in order to get their claws into him that they'd agree with most anything he said.

Kyle fired up the computer and leaned back, kicking his feet up onto the handmade wooden desk. He took another long taste of his beer, staring out into the night sky. The Denver skyline twinkled in the distance.

When his architect had suggested a full glass wall in the office, Kyle had thought the man a bit mad, but every night when he sat in this very spot, he knew he'd been wrong.

The man had been a genius.

Something about the view, the expanse of land and sky, the enormity of it all, kept Kyle grounded. The sight was a constant reminder of who he was—and how small he was—in the grand scheme of things.

His father would have loved this view.

Kyle's gut twisted. He'd never known his dad after his mother had taken Kyle back to the States as a kid. When he and Robert Prescott had reconnected a few short years ago, the relationship had been strained, but there'd been a bond that Kyle had never felt with his stepfather.

Stephen Turner was a good man, but a chasm of awkwardness existed between them that Kyle could never quite bridge.

His father had been another matter altogether. Robert Prescott had been bigger than life, at least in Kyle's eyes. When his plane had gone down on a trip to Spain, Kyle's playboy antics had spiraled out of control. And he'd let them.

Why not?

He had no reason to do anything else.

Robert's wife, Evangeline, had taken over Prescott Personal Securities with an icy resolve. Matter of fact, he'd never so much as seen his stepmother flinch after his father's death. For all he knew, she was secretly happy to find herself in the position of boss.

Marriage.

He took another drink and shook his head.

Based on what Kyle had seen, he was the smart one. Love 'em and leave 'em. That way no one stuck around long enough to get hurt, or produce offspring.

The computer blinked the entry screen for his pass code and he dropped his feet to the floor, pulling the chair close to the desk.

He had work to do.

He typed in his code and waited for the TCM welcome screen to appear.

Kyle had decided not to wait for Dwayne Johnson to return his call. There was no time like the present to search the files in case he'd "signed" more than one memo in absentia.

If someone had used his electronic signature, Kyle had every intention of finding out who…and why.

SARA BYPASSED the cubicles inside the Prescott Personal Securities headquarters and headed straight for Evangeline Prescott's corner office. She'd received a call from her boss on her secure line not long after Kyle's physician left.

Word had spread about the accident and Evangeline wanted a face-to-face. Like Sara, Evangeline didn't think the SUV's maneuvers had been anything but deliberate.

But why? And who?

Was Kyle Prescott the next name on the list of land investors in the TCM scheme? Had Sara merely been in the wrong place at the wrong time?

Or was the man a target for an altogether different reason?

Sara knew the collision hadn't been meant for her.

She hadn't been on the case long enough to raise anyone's interest. Had she?

She rubbed her shoulder absentmindedly as she tapped on the doorjamb to Evangeline's office. Her boss looked up and smiled, pushing herself to her feet.

Her long blond hair had been sleeked into a flawless twist and her vivid blue eyes sparkled through the reading glasses that sat partway down her nose. She pulled Sara into a quick hug, the move taking Sara by surprise.

Sara hadn't seen her parents in years, and she had no personal life to speak of, so the genuine display of affection was something she wasn't used to. It was also a side of Evangeline rarely witnessed.

"Thank goodness you're all right." Evangeline pushed Sara out to arm's length and smiled. She gestured to the sofa that sat facing the bank of windows overlooking downtown Denver. "Sit down. Can I get you something? Coffee? Water?"

Sara nodded. "Coffee sounds great."

She stared out into the lights of the city as Evangeline pressed the intercom. "Coffee please, Angel. And bring in the other items we discussed, if you would."

Sara narrowed her eyes suspiciously. "Other items?"

A smile tugged at one corner of Evangeline's mouth. "Secret weapon. You'll see." She sat down on the sofa and patted Sara's knee. "Start at the beginning and don't leave out a single detail."

Her expression turned from gentle to intense.

"You never know what's going to be the clue that breaks this investigation wide open."

Sara nodded and launched into a blow-by-blow description of the day's events. She left out nothing, even going so far as to detail the kiss she and Kyle had shared at the top of the mountain.

"Plates on the SUV?" Evangeline asked as soon as Sara stopped speaking.

"Wyoming." Sara shook her head. "I got the first three digits, nothing more."

Evangeline nodded and stood, reaching for the notepad on her desk. She handed it to Sara along with a pen. "Let's get it all down. We'll see what magic we can work with what you got."

A pang of sadness hit Sara as she remembered the man who would have had no trouble making the information sing. Only a few weeks had passed since Lenny had been senselessly murdered, and the sudden shock had begun to give way to acceptance and grief.

The man who had been PPS's resident computer genius was sorely missed. A geek among geeks, as he'd referred to himself. A true one-of-a-kind.

Sara wrenched her thoughts to the present. Surely someone else could make the database sing using just the SUV's description and the partial plate.

Sara had no sooner finished making her notations than a knock sounded at Evangeline's door.

Angel, one of the company's receptionists, entered, black hair gleaming and multiple piercings shining.

"You're all right?" she asked Sara, a note of genuine concern softening the harsh, Goth facade she maintained.

Sara nodded. "Thanks."

Sara's eyes, however, never left the object Angel carried. Two steaming mugs of coffee sat balanced on top of a large, flat box.

The secret weapon?

What on earth was Evangeline up to now?

Angel set the box on Evangeline's worktable, handed Evangeline and Sara each a mug, then looked at Evangeline. When Evangeline nodded, Angel carried the box to Sara and set it in her lap.

"Your secret weapon."

Sara's pulse quickened inexplicably. "What is it?"

"The key to my stepson's heart," Evangeline answered.

Sara studied the size and depth of the box. Lingerie perhaps? Her belly tightened at the very thought of modeling lingerie for Kyle Prescott. Their kiss had been hot enough to momentarily undo her focus. She didn't want to consider what a lingerie-modeling session might do.

She swallowed.

"Open it." Evangeline instructed.

Sara lowered her coffee mug to an end table then slipped her fingertips beneath the edges of the box, slowing lifting the lid.

A plate of brownies sat inside, carefully sealed in a clear container.

She squinted and frowned. "This is the secret weapon?"

Angel excused herself from the room as Evangeline softly chuckled. But when Sara lifted her gaze to that of her boss, Evangeline's blue eyes had gone steely.

"You've got to get inside his life." She patted the container of sweets. "Seems to me this would get you in the door of his home with no problem. Let him think you're the perfect little woman—intelligent and attractive, with a great cook on staff."

She tipped her chin toward the brownies then stood, moving back to her desk.

"We've received some new intel that's rather disturbing when it comes to my stepson. Seems you've edged your way into his life at the perfect time."

Sara set the container of brownies aside and straightened. "Like what?"

Evangeline nodded. "A series of real estate documents bearing his electronic signature. All pivotal to the land deals yet detrimental to TCM."

"I don't understand." Sara frowned.

"Even though the documents bear his signature, they point the finger of responsibility—and guilt— squarely at TCM. Quite brilliantly, actually."

"But why?" Sara ran the information through her brain. She couldn't envision the Kyle she'd met doing what Evangeline was saying he'd done.

Yes, the man was as arrogant as they came, but based on his actions after the accident, his heart was a whole lot bigger—and softer—than he let on.

Was he capable of plotting to take down his family's company? He didn't seem the type.

Evangeline shrugged. "Kyle never warmed to his stepfather. Maybe he's setting the man up for a fall." Her expression softened and the corners of her eyes turned sad. "He was never the same after his father's death. Who knows what he's capable of."

Sara stood and paced a tight pattern to the windows and back. "Or maybe someone's setting up Kylé."

Evangeline's pale brows climbed toward her hairline. "So I see it's true what they say about Robert's son."

"What's that?" Sara turned to face her boss.

"His charm is legendary."

Sara tensed defensively. "Trust me, I have no plans to fall for his charm. I'm just trying to see this situation from every possible angle."

"Something you do extremely well." Evangeline hesitated momentarily before she continued. "There's one more thing."

"What?" Sara asked.

"We found a notation in the last victim's date book. Seems he had a meeting scheduled with a K.P. before his untimely death. Unfortunately, he wasn't able to keep his appointment."

"Kyle Prescott." A mix of excitement and disappointment fired in Sara's belly. She'd found just the man she needed to unravel the mystery lurking behind the corporate facade of TCM, yet her gut didn't believe him responsible.

Evangeline stood, her usual nonverbal mode of dismissal. "I trust you'll take care of those bumps and bruises—" she nodded toward the container of brownies as Sara picked it up "—and put those to good use."

Sara mulled over Evangeline's words as she drove back toward her apartment. She couldn't picture Kyle Prescott sabotaging the family corporation, but she forced herself to take a mental step back.

She'd known the man for mere hours. Who knew what he was really capable of?

She shoved the inexplicable flash of disappointment out of her mind for the second time since Evangeline had given her the news.

What had she expected? That Kyle Prescott might be more than handsome packaging and a society pedigree? That he might be innocent of the illegal doings inside TCM?

Was she so naive she'd fallen for his legendary charm just as Evangeline had suggested?

Get a grip, Montgomery. Now.

There had obviously been no love lost between Kyle and his half brother, Peter. Perhaps Kyle was out to hurt TCM, if for no other reason than to sabotage Peter.

Sara had no trouble, however, in picturing Kyle being involved in the oil-investing scheme. After all, he'd out and out declared his support for developing and drilling open land.

The puzzle pieces began to circulate through her brain, her favorite part of the investigative process. Now all she had to do was worm her way fully inside Kyle's life—and inside TCM.

She patted the container of brownies on the passenger seat, then traced a finger over the address of the all-night dry cleaner Evangeline had recommended. She'd drop off Kyle's tux jacket and have it repaired, cleaned and pressed by morning.

Tomorrow she'd dazzle the man with her concern, caring and her secret weapon.

She planned to use Kyle for an item on her personal agenda, as well.

Finding her sister's killer.

Her gut told her Peter Turner might hold the key to the mystery she'd failed to unlock even after all this time.

Kyle's half brother made her skin crawl, but Sara needed to follow up on what he'd said about Annemarie.

As best Sara could figure, Peter Turner would have been a mere five or six years old at the time of Annemarie's death, but if he'd found her to be kind and patient, he might have trailed behind her at the last party she'd attended.

Maybe, just maybe, he'd seen something that would finally lead Sara to Annemarie's killer.

After all, there had been no notes in the investigative file about interviewing a child that fateful day.

If Peter Turner had seen anything, no one had taken notice. Perhaps the investigating officers had overlooked a vital piece of evidence. A key witness.

Sara wouldn't make that same mistake.

Access to his half brother made cozying up to Kyle Prescott very attractive. The fact Kyle himself might be neck-deep in the oil scheme justified whatever moves Sara needed to make to win the man over.

Sara always got her man.

This time would be no different.

Chapter Four

Sara winced as she settled onto the floor, bracing her back against the sofa. Her body had begun to ache from the accident—if one could call it that—and she was doing her best to rest now in anticipation of charming Kyle Prescott starting bright and early in the morning.

Evangeline had sent her home with copies of the documents to review and familiarize herself with. She was no expert at land acquisition, but the documents certainly made it clear that TCM—and more specifically, Kyle Prescott—were acquiring as much oil-rich land as possible.

She took a sip of the strong coffee she'd brewed and stole a glance at Angel's container of brownies.

Her stomach growled.

She hadn't had a thing for dinner and heaven knew the cupboards were bare. The cupboards in her apartment were always bare.

Sara flipped through several of the documents.

Newly registered deeds. Title searches. All bearing electronic signatures noted as belonging to Kyle Prescott.

According to the evidence sitting right before her eyes, Kyle had been one very busy man. Perhaps he'd used his playboy image and his absence from the TCM offices to carry out his land deals in private.

The thing was, according to the documents, a trust had been the acquiring party. Kingston Trust. Additionally, the documents listed only one party as the authorized signatory. Kyle Prescott.

Yet, PPS had learned through their investigation to date that TCM was the force behind Kingston Trust. They just hadn't yet uncovered who at TCM was pulling the strings.

As it had done back at PPS headquarters, her gut protested the thought Kyle might be the mastermind.

Sara did her best to ignore the sensation and continued to study the documents, the locations of the properties, the timing of the acquisitions.

If she were going to successfully use Kyle Prescott to infiltrate TCM and find out just what was going on, she needed to internalize every scrap of information she could get her hands on. Once she got inside TCM itself, she'd find a way to access the corporate files.

Sara shot another glance at the container of brownies, this time stretching until her fingers snagged the lip of the container. She pulled it to her side, pried open the lid, stared inside, then frowned.

She couldn't imagine giving these brownies to Kyle Prescott was going to be anything other than a terrible waste of brownies.

She lifted one from the carefully arranged order and took a bite, instantly moaning at the melt-in-your-mouth perfection. If anyone had ever told her multi-pierced, Goth poster-child Angel could bake like this, she'd have told them to go get their heads checked.

And she'd have been wrong.

Sara polished off the first brownie then reached for a second. A few moments later, she'd settled back into her work, the container tucked into her lap. After all, she had a lot of material to commit to memory tonight.

She refocused on Kyle, and on TCM.

She had no doubt she'd find the proof she needed inside the offices of TCM. With the right information, she'd crack the case wide open and uncover the names of the surviving investors before anyone else met his or her untimely demise.

And no matter what her gut thought of Kyle Prescott's guilt or innocence, the man was firmly entrenched deep inside the investment scheme.

After all—Sara patted the pile of documents now sitting on her lap—the evidence didn't lie.

She reached for another brownie as her mind shifted from Kyle Prescott to his half brother, Peter Turner.

She glanced up at the framed photo of Annemarie that held a place of prominence on her living room wall.

When Sara had joined the FBI, she'd promised herself she'd use her new skill set to finally crack open her sister's case. To date, she'd failed miserably, but the TCM investigation presented an unexpected opportunity.

With a little creative investigating, she could no doubt exploit the current case to pursue the old.

With any luck at all, she'd take down whomever had been responsible for her sister's murder at the same time she took down whomever had been behind the Kingston investors' murders.

She popped another brownie into her mouth and refocused on the documents before her.

After all, no one had ever said she wasn't a whiz at multitasking.

KYLE WORKED LONG and hard into the night, methodically searching through the TCM database of files and reports, looking for anything that would shed light on the cryptic voice mail he'd received.

He'd also checked his corporate voice mail to make sure a second message hadn't yet been received. The mailbox had been empty. At least that was some small measure of relief.

He still had time to dig.

Kyle made it a practice to never face a perceived opponent without full information on whatever it was the opponent alleged. This time would be no different.

He'd searched first on the caller's name, Jonathan

Powers. He'd found just one record and that had been a form memo welcoming a numbered investor to Kingston Trust Investments.

Kyle could only assume his search on Powers's name had somehow matched the numbered document. The man's actual name appeared nowhere on the document.

He frowned.

The document bore his electronic signature.

What on earth was a document dealing with an investment firm doing buried deep within the TCM system? Under Kyle's signature?

He searched next on Kingston Investments, finding several more welcome memos. All addressed by number. All with his signature.

He knew better than to print the documents. The system was geared to log any print commands. That was one red flag he had no intention of flying.

Not yet.

The memo Powers had called about must be more than a welcome memo. Whatever it was, it contained information Powers thought potentially damaging to TCM.

Where was it? What was it?

Kyle scrubbed a hand across his face and glanced at the small clock on his desk—3:00 a.m.

Typically, he'd be beyond exhausted after being on the computer for so long and so late, especially after the day he'd had, but the curiosity and anger

pulsing through him had worked wonders in keeping him awake.

He launched himself out of his chair and crossed
to the glass wall, leaning against the cool, slick panes.
He'd long since dressed, pulling on a favorite pair of
shorts and an old University of Colorado sweatshirt.

His image reflected back at him in the glass—
darkened by the early morning sky.

Frustration edged through him.

Had he been so neglectful at TCM that someone
honestly thought they'd get away with conducting
business under his electronic signature without him
catching on?

Short answer? Yes.

He hadn't set foot inside TCM walls in months.

To add even more fuel to the fire, using his electronic signature was easier than most people would
think. All someone needed were the brains to access
the log of private and public keys and the ability to
match the correct keys to the correct signature.

The signature itself was made up of a randomly
generated string of letters and numbers, different
each time the signature was applied. But anyone
doing business with TCM needed only to use the
software TCM operated and supplied to validate the
authenticity.

Kyle opened the program he'd long ago installed
on his system and ran each document through the
necessary steps for validation.

Every signature passed.

Damn.

Someone had lifted his signature and he'd never been the wiser.

The reality of what had happened led him directly back to where he'd started.

Dwayne Johnson.

Senior Vice President for International Rights.

Kyle had given the man his private signature key to make life easier, and Johnson had either used that key for his own purposes or he'd provided it to a third party.

Even more concerning was the reality that if Kyle's signature was on these memos, there was nothing to prevent his stamp of approval from appearing on an entire project or directive.

Just as Powers had alleged.

Kyle pushed away from the window and headed for the phone. If Johnson thought he could get away with whatever it was he had going on, he'd better think again.

Kyle punched Dwayne Johnson's private number into the phone, not caring that it was three o'clock in the morning and not caring that he'd already put one call in to the man.

A call that had apparently been ignored.

Kyle felt no surprise when Johnson's machine picked up. He wouldn't expect any different at this hour of the morning, and he had no plans to leave a polite message. No plans at all.

"Johnson." He spoke the name sharply and loudly when the beep sounded. "If you ever want to collect another paycheck, you'll answer this damned phone and you'll answer it now."

A loud noise sounded on the other end of the line as someone bobbled the receiver.

"Sorry. Sleeping," Johnson said.

Kyle could care less.

"I suppose you've been sleeping ever since you ignored my last message."

"No, I—"

Kyle didn't give the man a chance to utter another syllable. "If you know what's good for you, you'll be at my front door first thing this morning."

Silence beat across the line.

"With your explanation of why my electronic signature is on a series of welcome documents for investors in something called the Kingston Trust."

"You've got to be—"

"Listen to me," Kyle interrupted again. "You are the only person at TCM with access to my signature. If you didn't sign these documents, then you know exactly who did. Be here by nine o'clock. Or else."

Kyle slammed down the phone.

He shut down the computer, plucked the empty beer bottles from his desk and dropped them in the recyclables container as he passed.

He headed not for his bedroom, but for his workout room instead.

Sleep wouldn't come tonight.

He knew that from experience.

And if he wasn't going to be able to sleep, he'd have to do something else to defuse the tension knotting every muscle in his body.

The image of Sara Montgomery flashed through his mind's eye. Spending some quality time with the woman would definitely be one way to the defuse the tension, but based on the fiery spirit she'd shown, breaking down her defenses was going to take some time.

He pulled on a pair of running shoes, fired up the treadmill and stepped on as the machine kicked into high gear.

Before long, Kyle was running at top speed, pressing through the pain of yesterday's injuries.

He put in five miles then hit a hot shower.

By the time Dwayne Johnson arrived, Kyle planned to be calm, collected and ready.

Johnson would never know what hit him.

SARA TOOK A LONG SWALLOW of her favorite coffee, studied the empty brownie container and grimaced. The oven timer chimed and she crossed her fingers as she approached the kitchen.

She'd been forced to find an all-night convenience store that sold brownie mix in order to replace the batch she'd eaten.

She had to admit Angel's brownies had been like

none Sara had ever tasted before. And they'd certainly helped pass the time while she studied the files on Kyle Prescott.

She opened the oven and smiled at the sight of the tray inside. Her brownies might not be works of art, but they certainly looked edible enough. She reached for the pan and winced as her finger brushed the scalding hot tray.

She stepped back, searching her kitchen for any sign of an oven mitt. She spotted a pair hanging on the side of the fridge, then returned to the task at hand.

A few minutes later, the tray of brownies sat cooling on the counter. Sara had moved on to the bathroom, where she studied her tangle of still damp waves.

The run she'd taken this morning had done wonders to unknot the tension in her shoulders. The exercise couldn't hurt in the calorie department, either. A fleeting thought of how many brownies she'd consumed crossed her mind, but she shoved it away.

She had bigger things to worry about today. Check that.

Bigger people.

Namely, Kyle Prescott.

The image of his handsome face flashed through her mind. The way he'd had full command of those he spoke with at his stepfather's party and the way he'd cut off his half brother's line of inappropriate questioning.

Sara rubbed her lips, gently remembering the feel of Kyle's mouth pressed to hers.

Her belly gave a traitorous twist and she groaned. Just what she didn't need. An unwanted attraction to the man who stood for everything she loathed in life—money, the attitude it inspired and the spoiled ways of someone who'd had everything in life handed to him on a silver platter.

The genuine concern Kyle had shown after the accident battled with the thoughts racing through her brain, but she merely shook her head. She had no doubt the gentleness he'd shown after the accident had been the result of the fall he'd taken, nothing more.

The man's modus operandi was arrogance. That's what she had to prepare for.

Nothing else.

Her slim denim skirt hugged her hips and ended just above her knees, showing off several inches of skin between the hem and the top of her favorite boots. Butter-soft antique white leather, hand-painted and stitched to perfection, hugged her legs, the colorful design climbing either side of her calves.

She'd topped off her outfit with her favorite white blouse, classic yet tailored. Very tailored.

The seaming fit her to perfection, the cut of the shirt skimming the fullness of her breasts and tapering sharply to her waist, fitting her like a second skin.

A tasteful second skin.

Sara typically kept the shirt buttoned to her neck, but today she'd gone for a more relaxed look, leaving the top three buttons undone, exposing the smooth skin of her neck and chest. As she studied herself in the mirror, she toyed with the idea of popping an additional button.

No, no. She checked herself. A former debutante would not expose that much skin.

She smiled inwardly.

Once a deb, always a deb, she reminded herself.

Wasn't it better to leave a bit to the man's imagination?

Sara bent at the waist, tousled her hair, straightened, then finger-combed the waves into place.

She pasted on her best here-I-come-calling-with-brownies smile, momentarily crinkled her nose at the reflection, then studied her overall appearance.

Not bad. Not bad at all.

Let the games begin.

KYLE DIDN'T WAIT for Dwayne Johnson to knock before he jerked the heavy wooden door open. He'd heard the rumble of a vehicle's engine in the drive and had only been momentarily surprised to hear not one, but two car doors slamming shut.

He should have known Johnson would bring backup. The identity of the man who stood back next to the SUV was predictable as well.

Buddy Forman.

Head of security for TCM. A frustrated he-man wannabe if ever there was one.

"Gentlemen," Kyle said as he turned to brace his knee against the edge of the door, effectively blocking Johnson's entrance. "I'd invite you in, but this won't take more than a few moments."

He leaned forward, closing the space between his face and Johnson's, taking some small measure of satisfaction on spotting the slight sheen of perspiration that lined his second in command's upper lip.

"By the end of the day today, you will deliver every memo, letter and document you've ever put my name to without my permission, and you will provide the name and contact information for anyone to whom you've given my private key."

Instead of flinching, Johnson straightened, meeting Kyle's glare head-on. "I'll do no such thing, because I've done no such thing."

Anger surged in Kyle's gut. He reached up, grasping the collar of Johnson's jacket. Forman took a step forward, but Kyle held up his free hand.

"Down, boy." Kyle spoke the words sharply, leaving no room for misunderstanding. When Buddy continued to move closer, Kyle lifted his gaze to meet the man's steely expression. "Perhaps you haven't checked your organizational chart lately. This weasel might be one of your supervisors, but I own you. Understand?"

Buddy stopped his forward motion, but made no move to back away.

Kyle shifted his focus back to Johnson's now flushed face, dropping his voice low. "I don't know what you think you're up to, or who you're working for. I'm sure there's someone. I know you're not capable of orchestrating any of this yourself.

"Just focus on this," he continued. "End of day. Today. Here. Everything you've either put my name to or helped someone put my name to. Understood?"

Johnson's expression tensed. "I have no idea what you're talking about."

Kyle squinted. "Then you'd better get busy finding out."

He released Johnson's jacket and the man staggered backward.

"Maybe if you spent more time at your job, you might not need me to tell you what's going on." Johnson straightened and turned away.

Kyle grasped the man's arm and jerked him so close he could feel his breath. Anger pulsed through him now, his fury ignited by Johnson's flippant attitude.

"End of business today." Kyle narrowed his gaze, speaking each word slowly and deliberately. "And bring me everything on Kingston Investments. Everything."

Johnson jerked his arm free of Kyle's grip. "My pleasure."

Kyle mulled over Johnson's parting words as he watched the two men climb into the dark SUV and pull away, leaving a cloud of dust behind.

He flashed back on the dark SUV that had forced him off the road the night before.

Could it be?

A sliver of trepidation wove its way inside him and he reminded himself he had no idea of exactly what he'd stumbled upon.

Johnson was right, as much as Kyle hated to admit it.

If Kyle had paid more attention to his supposed position at TCM, he would know what was going on.

He shook his head and turned to step back inside.

No matter. It was never too late to start taking your responsibilities seriously. And Kyle intended to do just that starting right now.

THE MORNING SUN glinted against something as Sara approached Kyle's address. Something shiny. Something huge. Something that brought back a flash of memories from yesterday's accident.

A large, black SUV sat squarely in front of Kyle's home.

Sara could clearly make out the vehicle through the landscaping of Kyle's drive and she realized if she could see the vehicle so clearly, then the hulk of a man standing next to the SUV's bumper could no doubt see her car, should he turn around.

Her pulse quickened, as it always did whenever she faced an unexpected challenge.

She continued past Kyle's home until she was far enough down the road to be out of sight.

She was no doubt being overly dramatic. For all Sara knew, Kyle had a team of house cleaners at his home this morning.

A team of house cleaners with a very large bodyguard.

No.

She shook her head and cut the engine on her compact car. Leaving the brownies behind, she reached into the glove compartment for her weapon. She searched her outfit for a spot to tuck the gun and chose her waistband, anchoring the small pistol carefully at the small of her back.

Sara glanced both ways then dashed across the main road. She made her way slowly and methodically toward the access road to Kyle's property, working to keep view-blocking foliage between herself and the man standing in Kyle's drive.

As she neared, Sara heard voices. Two, to be exact. Kyle's voice was raised and sharp, his palpable anger unmistakable. The second voice was lower, softer, too garbled to understand what it was the man was saying.

"I'll destroy you, do you understand me?"

Kyle's words, however, rang clear and menacing. A frisson of unease crawled up Sara's neck. Had she incorrectly been swayed by the man's charm, just as Evangeline had said?

As she leaned around a stand of pines, she got a clear view of Kyle grasping the second man's collar, practically hoisting the man's feet off the ground.

She deftly reached for the cell phone holster on her belt and slipped the phone free, flipping it open and pressing the button to activate the camera.

She quietly snapped off shot after shot—of Kyle physically threatening the second man, of the second man's face as he turned to walk away, profile and face of the goon by the SUV as he turned to climb back into the truck.

Just before the SUV launched into motion, she clicked a photo of the license plate. This SUV was not the same truck that had run her and Kyle off the road.

Yesterday's truck had been a different manufacturer, a bit sleeker, and it had sported a Wyoming plate.

It couldn't hurt to have a shot of the truck, though, and to find out exactly how the vehicle was registered and to whom.

She saved the shot and tucked the phone back into its holster.

Dust and dirt flew as the truck barreled back toward the main road—the main road where Sara and her car were woefully exposed should the vehicle turn in her direction.

To her amazement and relief, the truck took the

opposite route, its rear bumper quickly fading from her sight.

Sara glanced back at Kyle's front door, surprised to find him still standing on the top step, staring at the spot where the truck had been parked.

As she watched, he squeezed his eyes shut momentarily. Without thinking, she slipped the phone out of its holder one more time and snapped off a photo before Kyle pulled himself out of whatever thoughts he was having.

His expression morphed from angry to frustrated to puzzled.

Sara frowned. A few moments before she would have bet the man was intent on murder, but now? Now he looked like a man who had found himself up to his neck in something he couldn't quite figure out.

As Sara tucked the phone away, Kyle ran a hand across his face and into his hair then turned. He stepped back into the house and pushed the door shut behind him.

Sara straightened, hurrying back toward her car.

Now that the coast was clear, she needed to shake herself back into her undercover role—former debutante on a house call with brownies, albeit from a box, in tow.

Try as she might, she couldn't force the exchange she'd just witnessed out of her mind.

Her gut instinct told her that something in what

she'd just seen and heard presented a key piece of evidence in her current investigative puzzle.

She flipped open her phone and pressed a series of keys, transmitting photo after photo to the PPS offices for identification.

Sara might be about to morph into the perfect picture of a Denver socialite, but there wasn't any reason why she couldn't launch some additional investigative work into action behind the scenes while she made nice with Kyle Prescott.

And nice was exactly what she intended to make.

For now.

Chapter Five

Kyle had just peeled off his T-shirt when the doorbell rang. If Johnson had returned, this time Kyle wouldn't let him get the last word before he walked away.

Kyle had been taken aback by the man's attitude, as if Johnson honestly didn't know what Kyle had been talking about. But surely Johnson had to be the one responsible for leaking Kyle's electronic signature access. Who else could it be?

Even though he'd run just a few hours earlier, Kyle had headed straight for his personal gym after Johnson left. Nothing in life cleared his head better than working up a good, old-fashioned sweat. Plus, the gym's view of the surrounding Red Rocks never failed to lift his spirits.

He reached for the front door and jerked it open without looking to see who was there.

Stunned silence hit him when he spotted Sara Montgomery, a Tupperware container in the crook of one arm, his tux jacket encased in a dry cleaner's bag in her other hand, and sunlight gleaming off the rich brown waves of her hair.

Her gaze blazed a trail down his bare chest then back up to meet his stare.

She wore a body-hugging denim skirt and white blouse that begged to be unbuttoned—slim-cut and nipped in at her shapely waist. She'd finished off the outfit with a pair of boots that left him staring at the curve of her calves.

"Catch you at a bad time?" A seductive smile tugged at the corners of her full lips as he redirected his gaze to her face.

Suddenly all thoughts of Dwayne Johnson and stolen electronic signatures fled Kyle's brain.

"Never a bad time for you," he answered. He pulled the door open wide. "Come in. Please. I'll go grab a clean shirt."

"Don't get dressed on my account." Sara raised her brows then held out the plastic container she'd been carrying. "Thought you might need something to nurse you back to health after yesterday."

Kyle took the container from her hands, feeling oddly self-conscious as her focus dropped to the still raw lacerations along his side.

"Did you have those looked at?" Genuine concern edged out the seductive tone that had filled her voice seconds before.

Kyle nodded. "Doc checked me out after he left

your house." He tipped his chin toward her side. "How are you feeling today?"

Sara gave a quick shrug. "I'll survive. I was worried about you, though. Did you call the police?"

Kyle stepped aside to let Sara enter his home. "Didn't see a point to it."

"What if it wasn't an accident?" Her eyes narrowed.

Kyle had never considered the incident anything close to an accident, but he wasn't about to say so to Sara.

He shook his head. "It's nothing I can't handle on my own."

He smiled then lightly touched the small of her back, guiding her into his foyer. Pleasure flooded through him at the look of approval that spread across Sara's lovely features as she took in his home.

He'd worked hard to achieve a blend of rugged and refined, doing his best to honor the home's majestic surroundings by using authentic materials and numerous windows to do the view justice.

Kyle had never worried about what other people thought of his actions or his belongings, but suddenly he cared what Sara thought.

"It's lovely." Her tone had gone soft, appraising. "Simply lovely."

"Can I offer you the grand tour?"

She nodded. "I'd like that very much."

He guided her through the living and dining areas, open in design with high, beamed ceilings. When they passed the galley kitchen, Sara tipped her chin toward the container Kyle still held, but hadn't yet opened.

"You might want to leave those here."

Damn. He'd been so taken with Sara he'd forgotten she'd handed him the gift.

Kyle set the container on the granite counter and pried open the lid. At least two dozen brownies lined the inside, stacked in a neat pattern of cut squares.

He smiled. "My favorite." Kyle lifted his gaze to study Sara's reaction. "How did you know?"

SARA SHRUGGED. "Lucky guess."

What was she going to say? *An elite team of investigators at the world-class PPS identified brownies as the secret weapon to gain access to your life?*

"Dig in."

Kyle's words jerked her attention back to the man standing before her, shirtless.

Much as she hated to admit it, the sight was more than a bit distracting. The man might have a reputation for avoiding office work, but he obviously embraced all things physical.

"No thanks—" Sara waggled a finger toward the brownies "—never touch the stuff."

More like she couldn't stomach the thought of ever eating a brownie again.

Kyle plucked a brownie from the container, took a bite and smiled. If Sara weren't mistaken his expression looked a bit forced.

All right, so she wasn't Betty Crocker…or Angel.

"Come on." Kyle gestured for Sara to follow him. "Let's finish the tour, then perhaps you'll let me take you out to breakfast."

Sara hesitated for only a moment. "Sounds perfect."

The thought of the extra time with Kyle was appealing on several levels, one of them being the chance to further question the man.

Kyle led her down a hallway, pointing out three large guest bedrooms and his master suite. The tour ended at his office, a spectacular room with a panoramic view Sara might have thought painted by a master, had she not realized she was looking through glass.

Sara walked to the transparent wall and gently touched her fingertips to the slick material.

"Was this your idea?" She glanced quickly over her shoulder at Kyle, then refocused on the view outside the home. "It's amazing."

He stepped close, so close she could almost feel the energy emanating off his body.

"I wish I could take credit, but this was the architect's idea."

"It's just like—"

Sara caught herself. She'd almost told Kyle the wall was just like the one in Evangeline's office.

That slip would have done wonders for her cover.

"It's just like something out of a magazine," she said instead. "Great view."

When she turned to face Kyle, she found him staring directly into her eyes instead of through the glass at the world outside.

"Isn't it, though?" he asked.

An unfamiliar urge to squirm filled Sara but she fought it. She'd never let a target unnerve her, and she wasn't about to start now.

She pointed to Kyle's bare chest. "Perhaps you should grab that shirt before we head out to breakfast."

A lopsided grin tugged at the lines of Kyle's mouth. "Give me ten minutes to shower and dress and I'll be ready to go."

Sara followed him back to the living area.

"Make yourself at home," Kyle said. "I'll be right out."

She waited until the sound of the shower filled Kyle's expansive home. She moved stealthily, but with purpose, back toward the office.

Now was the perfect time to assess the lay of the land, so to speak.

She paused at the doorway for a brief moment to make sure she still heard the shower running, then stepped inside.

Sara's breath caught once more at the sight before her. The line where the plains met the majestic beauty of the Red Rocks was beyond beautiful.

She shook herself out of her momentary trance.

Kyle had said ten minutes. She had to move quickly.

Sara reached instinctively for Kyle's computer,

pleased to see the stand-by button flashing. With the touch of the mouse, the screen blinked to life and Sara went to work, moving expertly to the list of most recently viewed documents.

Welcome memos.

Kingston Trust.

An odd mix of excitement and disappointment tangled inside her. Excitement that she'd found evidence tied to her investigation, but disappointment at the realization Kyle truly was involved in the conspiracy.

What about the murders?

Based on his display of temper a bit earlier, he might very well be capable.

Sara squeezed her eyes shut. She needed to focus solely on Kyle Prescott, the target, and not on Kyle Prescott, the man.

Sara had opened only the first memo when she heard footfalls in the hallway.

Damn.

What had the man done? Taken a two-minute shower?

She scanned the document, taking note of two things. The memo had been addressed not by name, but by number. She muttered softly.

That was not going to help her uncover the list of investors.

In addition, the document had been signed, albeit electronically, by none other than Kyle himself.

Son of a gun.

She deftly closed the document and programmed the computer to return to stand-by mode, praying the screen went black before Kyle cleared the doorway.

She launched herself away from the desk toward the spectacular view outside the window. Her heart pounded as she stood at the full-glass wall, fueled by a combination of nerves and excitement.

Just how many investors had received welcome memos from Kingston Trust and Kyle Prescott? How many more, still alive, might be targets for the land conspiracy? And was there some way to match the numbered memos to the series of land coordinates on the disk back at PPS headquarters?

She had to get back inside that computer. But how?

When Kyle cleared his throat behind her, she knew exactly what she had to do. She'd charm the pants off the man—literally—if that's what it took to get more time inside his home.

Their time together today was her opportunity to ingratiate herself into Kyle Prescott's world, and his life.

"See anything you like?"

Sara braced herself and squeezed her eyes shut momentarily at the sound of Kyle's voice.

Forcing a smile, she turned to meet his gaze, finding his expression serious, his brows furrowed.

So much for stealth.

Kyle wore a pair of faded blue jeans and a denim shirt, open at the throat. He'd rolled up the sleeves, and

Sara might be inclined to give him points for dressing so rebelliously, had he not sported what appeared to be a two-thousand-dollar Gucci wristwatch.

"This view." She jerked her thumb over her shoulder. "I had to see it again. I didn't think you'd mind." She stepped toward him, grazing her fingertips against the denim of his sleeve as she passed, headed toward the hallway. "My apologies."

"Accepted." He pulled the door shut behind him as he followed her across the threshold.

"Quick shower." Sara gave the man a head-to-toe appraisal. "Impressive."

A crooked smile pulled at the corner of Kyle's mouth. "I realized I didn't offer you anything to drink. I didn't want a well-mannered woman such as yourself to think me uncouth."

"Never." Sara closed the space between them, embracing her role fully. She stopped just short of where Kyle stood and widened her gaze. "I can think of many things I might think you, Mr. Prescott, but uncouth certainly isn't one of them."

"Very well, then." Kyle extended his hand and Sara took it, ignoring the jolt the contact sent through her system. "Let's get you some breakfast, shall we?"

AS HE DROVE TOWARD the outskirts of the city, Kyle considered the possible explanations for what had just happened.

Had Sara been snooping in his office?

Or had she legitimately been enjoying the view? A view she'd no doubt seen countless times as a lifetime Denver resident.

The Montgomery family had been part of the Denver social scene for as long as he could remember. Yet, he didn't recall seeing Sara before, and he would have remembered her if he had.

His brother, Peter, had apparently known the sister. He'd have to ask around a bit. Figure out exactly what Sara Montgomery was up to.

Maybe she'd been searching in his office for financial statements. After all, she wouldn't be the first woman to check the balance in his checkbook before proceeding with her seduction.

Wasn't that the first thing these women learned in preparation for their coming-out parties?

Sara Montgomery needn't worry. Kyle was loaded, but he had no intention of sharing. Marriage was not in the cards for him.

Casual diversions? Yes.

Commitment? No.

Was that the reason Sara had appeared on the scene—and more specifically in his life—now? Was she out to seduce him?

He talked himself out of the idea almost as quickly as he'd talked himself into it.

Sara Montgomery didn't fit the mold, and he knew the mold.

The woman was up to something else, but what?

A thought nagged at the base of Kyle's brain.

Sara had appeared the same day he'd received the mysterious message from Jonathan Powers.

What if she were somehow involved with the investor? Or working for the investor?

Maybe she hadn't been after financial statements at all. Maybe she'd been after the same thing Kyle had searched for last night.

Computer records.

He swore softly under his breath.

"Are you all right?" Sara's question sliced through his concentration.

"Just thinking about something back at the house," he answered. "Sorry about that."

"No problem."

Sara turned her attention back to the passing scenery and Kyle checked their location. Almost there.

He was no doubt imagining a threat where there was none, but he needed to be cautious just the same.

Sara Montgomery was probably nothing more than a woman on the prowl, but just in case she was far more, he'd keep his guard up.

As much as the beauty turned his head and dulled his focus, he couldn't afford any missteps, not until he knew exactly what he was dealing with.

SARA RECOGNIZED the sweeping beauty of the Red Rocks as they approached.

She sighed inwardly, again remembering how

Annemarie had loved to explore the area attractions, and goodness knew there were many. Just none that Sara had visited since her sister's death.

Kyle pulled his Esplanade into the parking area and cut the engine.

"Ever been to the Ship Rock Grille?"

His eyes met hers and for the briefest moment she saw something more there than she'd seen before. A question? A doubt?

Sara ignored her curiosity and gave a quick shake of her head. "No."

She stayed seated as Kyle climbed out of the driver's seat, resisting the urge to open the passenger door, waiting instead for Kyle to open it for her.

He took her hand as she stepped down from the truck, and Sara once again noticed the roughness of Kyle's firm touch. Not what she would have expected based on the man's playboy reputation.

Their conversation was sparse during their meal, as if they both had other things on their mind than polite small talk.

Sara mentally scolded herself. She couldn't afford to waste this time alone with Prescott doing anything other than digging herself deeper into her cover.

She'd have to work harder, and as they stepped outside into the crisp June air, she set her sights on doing just that.

As they headed toward the rugged expanse of the Red Rocks Amphitheatre, Sara felt the increasing pressure of both the investigation and Anne-marie's memory.

"My sister and I used to come here." Her heart ached as she remembered. "We'd stand on the stage and sing our hearts out. Best acoustics in the world, they say."

Kyle stood in silence for several beats, studying her. Sara dipped her head when the length of their locked gaze grew uncomfortable.

"I would have liked to have seen that," he said, tucking his hands into the pockets of his jeans and climbing up several rows of seats.

Sara followed, imagining the space filled with the over nine thousand people the amphitheatre could seat. She suddenly felt more alone than she'd felt in years.

"Were you close?" Kyle asked.

Sara raised her brows in question.

"You and your sister."

Sara nodded. "Very."

"It must have been very difficult for—"

"It was," Sara interrupted him.

She'd promised herself a long time ago she was done with the pity. Done with the sympathy. There was no reason to dredge up the old emotions now.

She continued up the steps, passing Kyle.

"I can't believe anyone would want to develop a single inch of what's out there."

Sara gestured to the expanse of open plains that spread as far as the eye could see, hoping to change the subject. Before them sat nothing but land and sky until the distant skyline of Denver broke the line of the horizon.

"I lied."

Kyle's words stopped Sara cold. She turned to face him. "About what?"

"The land development." His lips pressed into a tight smile and she couldn't help but notice his laugh lines, as if he'd lived a lifetime of happiness. "I lied." He shrugged, passing her on the steps.

"You don't support the development?" Her voice climbed in disbelief.

Kyle slowed long enough to grin at her over his shoulder. "I despise it. I wanted to see if you'd give the typical response of the rich and powerful."

He gestured toward the top of the amphitheatre. "Come on. You passed."

"What about the oil?" Sara called out after him.

"What about it?" Kyle shrugged. "Maybe it's time we learned another way to fuel our lifestyles."

Sara watched his back as he put more and more distance between them. Kyle's words didn't jibe with those of a man involved in a scheme to buy up oil-rich land.

Was he on to her?

Was he telling her this to put her off his trail?

Maybe he'd realized it wasn't the view she'd been admiring in his office.

She launched herself into motion.

Kyle Prescott's words weren't what she needed to

focus on right now. She needed to focus on his actions, and on the actions of the powers that be at TCM.

Her role today was to figure a way inside the monster company's operations.

In the meantime, she'd content herself with finding a way back inside Kyle's home office…and his computer.

Chapter Six

Starved after spending the day playing tourist, Kyle and Sara had settled for a fast-food drive-thru on the way home. Sara laughed inwardly at the sight before her as they sat at his dining room table.

Two flawless crystal glasses filled with what was no doubt exquisitely expensive Pinot Noir kept their fast-food hamburger wrappers company.

So much for high society.

A tight laugh slipped between her lips.

"Something funny?" Kyle grinned as he asked the question and Sara did nothing more than cast a glance toward the spread on the table. Kyle shrugged. "It was either this or I dazzle you with my cooking."

The phone rang before Sara could answer, but Kyle ignored the sound.

He shook his head as he dug into the pile of French fries sitting between them. "The machine can get it. I wouldn't want to let my meal get cold."

But when the harsh male voice sounded after

Kyle's outgoing message, Kyle launched himself to his feet and out of the room without so much as excusing himself.

Sara picked up the name *Johnson* in the message and she most definitely picked up the words *or else* before Kyle silenced the machine.

Not exactly what she'd consider a friendly phone call.

Kyle returned almost immediately, but the playful light in his vivid eyes had been extinguished, replaced instead by a cold veil.

Had the voice on the machine been Dwayne Johnson looking to continue their argument from earlier that day?

Sara had received positive identification on the photos she'd sent in to headquarters. Angel had text-messaged her Evangeline's response and Sara had been able to review the information earlier that day during one of her bathroom visits.

The smaller of the two had been Dwayne Johnson, the man behind Kyle Prescott at the helm of TCM's international rights division.

The second man—the behemoth—had been Buddy Forman, head of TCM security. A fitting job for a man of his size if ever there were one.

Based on the intensity of Kyle's glare, he couldn't wait to return Johnson's call. The time had come for Sara to call it a day, but not before she did one more thing.

If Kyle planned to speak with Dwayne Johnson, Sara planned to hear every word. She knew exactly what she needed to do. She simply needed to create a small diversion.

She patted the restaurant napkin to her lips and excused herself from the table. "I should probably get going." She reached for her purse. "I'll just freshen up first, if you don't mind."

Kyle gave a distracted shake of his head, a far cry from the attentive man he'd been all day.

Once inside Kyle's bathroom, Sara pulled her cell from her purse and speed-dialed Evangeline's private number, breathing a sigh of relief when the woman answered on the third ring.

"I need you to call your stepson, but not on his home line. On his cell."

Silence beat between them, not surprising in the least. Evangeline was typically short on chitchat but long on details.

"He's received a phone message from Johnson and I need to tap into his line before they speak," Sara explained.

"You have the tools you need?" Evangeline's crisp words carried across the line.

"Always." Sara nodded as she spoke, as if Evangeline could see her.

"Five minutes?"

"Perfect."

Sara disconnected the call and flushed the toilet

for good measure. She washed her hands, fluffed her hair in the mirror and reapplied her lipstick.

After all, she might as well look the part of interested suitor.

She reached into a zippered compartment of her purse and removed two items—the tiny electronic listening device PPS had developed for just such an occasion, and the set of tools she'd need to complete the job.

She slipped both items into her boots and stepped out into the hall.

Kyle's cell phone rang just as she reached the dining room.

He frowned as he read the caller ID, but snapped open the phone just the same.

"I'm with someone, I'll have to call you back."

The terse note in his voice was one Sara hadn't yet heard and she reminded herself that she had no right to be surprised. Spending one day with a man did not provide full access to his true self.

Kyle's frown deepened as he listened to whatever Evangeline was saying. He shot an apologetic glance at Sara and held up one finger.

She nodded, holding her breath as he stepped out of the room.

Don't go in your office. Don't go in your office.

Much to her relief, he headed for the front door and stepped outside.

Sara didn't waste any time.

She slipped into his office, this time looking away from the magnificent view and lights of downtown Denver twinkling in the distance. She reached for the phone, tracing the incoming line to the wall jack, then dropping to her knees.

She reached into her left boot and extracted the tiny device she'd stashed there. She next slipped her favorite gadget—her multitool system—from her right boot.

She ran her fingertip along the edge of the small item, over the various bumps and ridges of the assortment of tools, settling on the one she needed now. The tiny Phillips head screwdriver.

With a practiced ease, she unfastened the two screws holding the plate covering the phone line and lowered the ceramic piece to the floor. She stopped to listen. Nothing.

Sara next unclasped the electronic bug and reached for the red phone wire, pulling a length long enough to grip between her fingers. She positioned the listening device on the wire and squeezed it shut, smiling with satisfaction at the click the two halves made as they joined together.

In less than twenty seconds, she'd tucked the wire back into place and replaced the faceplate. She kept the tiny tool gripped in her fist as she hurried back toward the dining room table, doing her best to move silently across the expansive hardwood floor.

Sara had no sooner dropped the tool back into her purse and picked up her wineglass than the front door opened and Kyle reappeared.

"Everything all right?" she asked.

"Just perfect." The light quality of his voice belied the tense lines of his face. "My stepmother needed a few answers with regard to my father's estate."

"Are you two close?"

Kyle shook his head. "Not particularly."

She wasn't surprised by the answer. Evangeline rarely mentioned Robert's son and when she did it was with a note of disdain. From what Sara gathered, there had been no love lost between the two.

"I'm sorry," she said softly.

Kyle's dark brows drew together.

"For your loss," Sara continued. "It's not easy to lose someone you love. To go forward."

Kyle sank onto the chair next to her. "We never had much of a chance to know each other." He raked a hand through his hair and Sara found herself once again wondering just how much styling went into the perfect, yet unkempt, look. "My father and I hadn't seen each other in a long time."

Sara set her wineglass on the table and stood. "I should be going. I know you've got calls to return."

A look passed across Kyle's face and Sara tried her best to decipher the expression.

Disappointment? Relief?

Kyle stood and took her hand, enveloping Sara's

slender fingers inside his solid grip. "Thank you for today."

A palpable tension beat between them. Sara had to forcibly remind herself that Kyle Prescott was not only her target, he was also a younger, perfect example of the life she'd long ago sworn off.

Before he could make any move to kiss her, Sara pulled her fingers from his and reached for her purse.

"I should thank you. It was wonderful to go visit the old sites."

Kyle walked her to the door and stood watching as she climbed into her car and cranked the engine. He didn't step out of sight until she was more than halfway to the main road.

Sara shoved all thoughts of the day out of her head and focused. She turned left and pulled into the same secluded spot she'd used that morning.

She snapped on the car's radio and pressed the tuning button until the numbers displayed the proper frequency for the bug she'd planted. Silence.

Perfect.

Kyle hadn't yet returned Dwayne Johnson's call. When he did, she'd be listening.

KYLE WAITED a polite amount of time before he shut the door on Sara's departing car. While he would have enjoyed having more time together to relax and drink their wine, her sudden departure wasn't a bad thing.

The day had most definitely been an enjoyable

one even though her attendance at his stepfather's birthday party had begun to nag at him.

Kyle dragged a hand through his hair and shoved the suspicious thought out of his mind. Right now he needed to get to the bottom of whatever was going on at TCM.

Uncovering Sara Montgomery's true motivation could wait.

He had to return Johnson's call and find out what in the hell the man was talking about.

He made a quick stop in the kitchen to snag a beer then headed straight for his office. He sat on the corner of his desk, staring out into the crystal clear Colorado night as he dialed Johnson's number.

An answering machine picked up after the first ring and Kyle swore under his breath.

He barely gave the machine time to beep before he spoke. "It's Prescott. Pick up."

A distinct click sounded on the other end of the line. He heard Johnson breathe before the man answered, the sound setting Kyle's teeth on edge.

"You got my message?" Johnson asked.

"I told you to be here in person," Kyle answered. "I suppose you're proud of your handiwork?"

Johnson's voice sounded tight, his breathing labored, as if the excitement of whatever he'd discovered had been too much for his system to handle.

"I have no idea what you're talking about."

"You're going to tell me you don't remember signing the memos? The target assessment requests? The purchase directives?"

Countless thoughts swirled through Kyle's mind. "What are you talking about?"

"You can play dumb with me, Prescott, but your stepfather and the rest of the executive board aren't going to buy your act."

Kyle squeezed his eyes shut, racking his brains to make sense of Johnson's blathering.

"You're the only one with my private key. If my signature's there, you put it there."

"That's where you're wrong," Johnson answered. "I had to dig deep to find these files. No one's going to find them unless I tell them where to look.

"Nice job," Johnson continued. "This is going to destroy your stepdaddy's company when it comes out, not to mention what it will do to you and everyone else involved."

Kyle reached for his computer, clicking a key to wake the machine from hibernation.

"I can keep my mouth shut about this—" Johnson's tone sent a cold chill down Kyle's spine "—but it's going to cost you."

"Cost me?" Kyle tucked the phone against his neck and punched in the command to access the TCM system.

He tried to pull up the file that had contained the welcome memos the night before, frowning when the system was slow to return the list.

"Did you screw with the records when you were in the system?" Kyle asked, working feverishly to make the machine produce the documents he'd requested.

Johnson's laugh filtered across the line, cold and heartless. "So you do know what I'm talking about then. I'll be in touch."

"I'm warning you, Johnson, if you—"

The phone clicked dead in Kyle's ear.

It's going to cost you.

His second in command's words rang in his ears. Kyle had never heard the man sound so determined or focused.

Whatever he had found on Kyle must be huge, and serious enough to take down TCM.

Well, if Johnson wouldn't come clean about the details there was only one thing for Kyle to do.

Find them himself.

SARA SAT in stunned silence after the listening device's transmission stopped.

She waited for several minutes, just to make sure she remained in range should Kyle make a second call. When nothing happened, she turned the ignition key and pulled back onto the road, trying to digest what she'd just overheard.

Dwayne Johnson had apparently uncovered clear documentation of the land conspiracy. Documentation implicating Kyle. And the man was prepared to blackmail Kyle in return for his silence.

The piece of the puzzle that nagged at her was Kyle's reaction.

Either he deserved an Academy Award for his performance or he actually hadn't known what Johnson was talking about.

Was it possible that Kyle's signature had been used without his knowledge?

But then he'd said something in direct opposition to the surprise he'd expressed.

Did you screw with the records when you were in the system?

Maybe the reason the welcome memos had been the most recently accessed documents on his computer was that he'd been doing some fishing himself, trying to figure out what was going on.

Could it be?

As she headed back toward downtown Denver and her apartment, Sara realized she now had more questions than she had answers, but one thing was crystal clear....

If Kyle were involved, Sara had to get back inside his office and into his computer before he or someone else had a chance to delete the evidence.

She needed her rest.

Tomorrow promised to be a busy day.

KYLE WORKED the TCM system for hours, butting up against security wall after security wall. For the life of him, he couldn't remember having to clear this many access layers in order to get deep inside the company records.

No wonder Johnson had said finding the records had taken quite a bit of work.

When Kyle's gaze landed on a file folder labeled Kingston Investments, his gut caught.

Bingo.

The hunting excursion had taken some time, but the sight that met him when he double-clicked the folder blew him away.

Document after document, sorted by what appeared to be land coordinates.

He clicked on the first subfolder then opened a window for each of the documents inside.

One target assessment for a large parcel of land outside city limits.

Hidden potential analysis for the same.

An offer of agreement for sale.

Kyle frowned.

Each document had been coded by number. Not a single investor or property owner name had been listed.

Since when had TCM gotten into bed with an investment firm, let alone an investment firm buying up property? And why the need for such anonymity?

He scrolled to the signature box on the target assessment, holding his breath as he did so.

"Son of a—"

He blew out the words on a frustrated breath.

Kyle Prescott.

His typed name and electronic signature loomed big as life on the document.

"I'll be damned."

Kyle had no idea of exactly who had been behind the massive trail of paperwork that spread across the screen in front of him, but one thing was for certain. Whoever it was had set out to paint Kyle as the mastermind behind the entire operation, and they'd apparently done a thorough job.

Kyle took a long drink from his beer then pulled his chair in close. He reached into his desk drawer for a tablet and a pen.

Before the night was through he planned to make note of every single piece of evidence against him that lurked in the TCM system.

He shook himself into focus and dragged a hand across his face.

According to the list of files and folders before him, it was going to be a very long night.

Chapter Seven

Kyle wasn't surprised by the shocked expressions as he walked through the doors of TCM bright and early the next morning.

Quite frankly he was surprised the staff remembered him at all. Of course, when your image smiled front and center in the family portrait hanging in the lobby, people had a tendency to recognize you for who you were.

He headed first for the kitchen area and a large cup of coffee, then directly for his office suite. He took the long route around the executive area in order to avoid both his stepfather's office and that of his half brother, Peter.

He suspected one or both of them might somehow be involved in the Kingston documentation he'd found, and he had no intention of facing either one of them until he'd cornered Johnson and searched the hard-file copies.

When Kyle barged through the door of Dwayne

Johnson's office a few moments later, he stopped cold in his tracks.

Empty.

Desk devoid of any sign of work.

According to company legend, Johnson hadn't missed a day of work in over fifteen years. The man was loyal, hardworking and had tunnel vision. A man so devoted to Stephen Turner he'd walk off a cliff should the TCM CEO ask him to do so.

Yet Kyle knew better.

Dwayne Johnson was apparently willing to sell out that loyalty without a second thought—for the right price.

Stephen had expected Kyle to be grateful when Johnson had been made his second in command at International, but Kyle had felt nothing more than manipulated. He knew when he was being watched, and when he was being babysat.

Dwayne Johnson was a master at both.

Kyle pulled Johnson's office door shut behind him and trailed his fingers across the spotless—and empty—desk. His gaze dropped to matching file drawers on either side of the desk, then to the credenza centered below the office window.

If Johnson wasn't here, there was really only one way to proceed.

Kyle tried one file drawer, then the other.

Locked.

While he hadn't expected Johnson to be absent, he had expected any file drawers to be locked.

He'd come prepared.

Kyle slipped a tiny key from his suit jacket pocket and fit it into Johnson's desk drawer. With a bit of finesse, the lock turned and the drawer slid open freely.

After all, there was nothing illegal about accessing your own family's records, right?

Kyle pressed the intercom button on Johnson's phone, waiting until the department executive assistant spoke.

"Darlene?"

Her stunned silence stretched across the line. "Mr. Prescott?"

Kyle let the chuckle slide between his lips. "You sound as though you've heard a ghost."

"Yes, sir."

He refocused, his tone going intent and serious. "Any word from Johnson today? I'm in his office and he's most definitely not here."

"No, sir. He hasn't called in, and I'm not showing any appointments in his book."

Kyle frowned. "That's odd, isn't it?"

"Very odd, sir."

Johnson might be the most annoying man Kyle had ever had the privilege to know, but he was reliable. If something had come up in the man's personal life, he'd have called Darlene. Based on the threatening tone of his call the night before, Kyle could only think of one thing.

The man had taken the evidence against TCM and Kyle and he'd gone underground.

"Track him down for me, would you, Darlene? It's urgent."

"Right away, sir."

Kyle released the intercom button and sank into Johnson's chair.

Johnson may have taken the evidence and run, but Kyle had zero intention of leaving the man's office until he'd checked every nook—he jiggled his key in the second lock and the door popped open—and cranny.

SARA STRAIGHTENED under the watchful gaze of Evangeline Prescott and finished recounting the details of the evening before.

Evangeline said nothing, and the other agents gathered in the small conference room followed her lead, remaining quiet, simply watching Sara.

"Next steps?" Evangeline asked.

"I have to get back inside his office," Sara replied, pulling herself taller in her chair.

"Or into TCM offices." Angel spoke from the doorway where she stood holding a tray of baked goods in her arms. She shrugged, a depressing vision in head-to-toe black, piercings gleaming in the morning sun. "I couldn't sleep last night. So, I baked."

"If you want me to pass those off as coming from me—" Sara studied the assortment of scones and muffins "—you can forget it. He'd never believe me."

Angel smiled expectantly at Sara. "How did he like my brownies?"

Sara thought about telling a small fib, but she didn't have it in her. "They never made it to his house. I made my own."

A collective groan went up from the small group and Sara cast a glare at those gathered. Before she could say a word, Evangeline interrupted.

"Place those on the table, Angel." She tipped her perfectly coiffed head toward the center of the room. "Thank you. That will be all for now."

Angel nodded, set down the tray and left.

One of Evangeline's pale brows lifted toward her hairline. "Help yourself, team. Maybe an influx of carbohydrates will loosen up our thought processes."

"I know what I need to do," Sara explained as the other agents reached for the tray. She longingly watched as the number of available pastries rapidly diminished, but she kept her focus trained on the case, and Kyle Prescott.

"If Kyle Prescott is behind the documentation, I'll be able to find additional records within his system," she continued. "The memo I found wasn't on his hard drive, it was on a virtual private network he'd tapped into."

"TCM's?" Evangeline asked.

Sara nodded. "Exactly."

"And how do you propose to garner an invitation back inside his home?"

"I plan to invite myself." Sara gave a quick lift and drop of her shoulders. "I left my lipstick in his bathroom. I'm sure I'm not the first woman to do so, and I won't be the first to drop by just to give a quick look for it."

A subtle smile pulled at Evangeline's lips and the other agents gathered shook their heads.

The reality was that Sara rarely wore much more than moisturizer, so the irony of her plan wasn't lost on her team.

The Sara they knew wouldn't give a second thought to a lost tube of lipstick, nor would she plant such an item in order to get into a man's home. But Sara Montgomery, upwardly mobile society wanna-be, would very well do exactly that.

"I do need one thing researched for me." Sara leveled her eyes at Evangeline. "I need to know how someone might go about stealing an electronic signature—or duplicating one."

Evangeline's gaze narrowed. "You still think Kyle might be innocent, don't you?"

Sara shook her head as she stood. "Just looking at all the angles, Evangeline." She shot a knowing smile over her shoulder as she stepped out of the office and headed back toward her undercover role. "Just like you taught me."

KYLE BREATHED a sigh of relief as he stepped back into his home. Spending most of the day at TCM had been taxing on a variety of levels.

Once word had leaked that he was in the building, Peter had dogged his every move, making an additional search of Dwayne Johnson's office impossible.

There had been one saving grace.

Kyle had managed to get through his entire visit without running into his stepfather.

He shrugged out of the cashmere blazer he'd worn to the office and plucked the house phone from its base. He flipped through the stored numbers that had been dialed, punching the redial button when he hit on Johnson's.

The man's machine picked up on the first ring, just as it had done the night before, but this time, when Kyle instructed Johnson to pick up, nothing happened.

"I know where to find you, Johnson." Kyle's voice rose with the anger and frustration he'd held bottled inside since his discovery last night. "You can't hide forever, and if you're behind this, you will pay. Trust me on that one."

He pressed the disconnect button and threw the phone at the sofa.

The ring of the doorbell startled him, sending adrenaline dancing to life in his veins.

A mixture of surprise and suspicion battled for

position inside him when he opened the door to find Sara Montgomery standing on his step.

She held up two large paper sacks, one in each hand. "Dinner is served."

Kyle smiled reflexively. "To what do I owe the pleasure?"

Sara tipped her head to one side as she entered, sending her brown waves swinging. "I wanted to say thank-you for such a lovely day yesterday." She hesitated for a moment and flashed a smile that stole Kyle's breath away. "And I think I left my favorite lipstick in your bathroom."

Kyle laughed. "No one could ever accuse you of being less than honest, Ms. Montgomery."

The smile on Sara's lips faltered for a split second, and Kyle couldn't help but wonder if his honesty comment hadn't hit a nerve.

He nodded toward the bags. "What culinary delight have you brought me today?"

Sara headed straight for the kitchen, looking as though she'd made the walk countless times before and fit seamlessly into Kyle's home and life.

He shoved the thought out of his head.

He might enjoy the woman's company, but sooner or later she'd move on. They all did once he made it clear he had no plans to marry. Not now. Not anytime in the future.

"Sushi," Sara called back as she began to hoist containers out of the bag and spread them across the kitchen island. She plucked two pairs of chopsticks from the bag, separated the halves and held out a pair to Kyle. "You game?"

Kyle's body responded to the pull of Sara's sweater across her breasts as she leaned forward, and to the curve of her waist where the soft fabric disappeared into the waistband of her hip-hugging jeans.

He reached for the chopsticks, capturing her hand in his as he did so. "I'm always game."

SARA SNAPPED LIDS back onto the uneaten portion of their dinner as Kyle explained what it had been like to come back to the States after being separated from his father for so long.

As objective as she was trying to be, her heart went out to the man.

He made no pretense about whether or not his upbringing had been happy, just as he made no pretense about the strained relationship he now had with his mother and her husband.

It was his half brother, Peter, about whom he avoided all of Sara's inquiries.

"I didn't know her." Kyle shrugged as he answered Sara's question about Annemarie. "Peter must have, but he would have been very young." He lifted his gaze to hers and their eyes locked for several tension-filled moments. "If she looked anything like you, I would have remembered. Sorry."

Annemarie.

Sara shoved down the old hurt, trying to focus on why she was really here tonight inside Kyle's home. She needed to get back into his office and his system, tempting as it was to pump him for information about the past and about his family's knowledge of Annemarie.

She had faith that the time would come to pursue her own investigation, and when it did, she'd be ready.

Kyle stepped close and lifted the container Sara held from her hands. He took both of her hands in his, then smiled.

"It's a gorgeous night. Let's sit outside. These will keep."

Unmistakable attraction arced between them.

Sara felt it in the tightening of her belly and the warmth that spread up her cheeks as Kyle held her hands. She read the mutual attraction in the darkening of Kyle's eyes and the softening of his features.

Kyle reached for her, cupping her chin gently in his fingers and running his thumb across her bottom lip, so softly Sara thought she might have imagined his touch. Based on the lump tightening in her throat, he'd definitely touched her. And she'd definitely responded.

"Maybe for just a little while." She spoke the words softly.

The sight that greeted her when Kyle led her outside momentarily stole her breath.

Soft, inground lighting illuminated a terra cotta patio with a sweeping view of the surrounding area.

For the briefest moment, Sara wanted to lose herself in the sensation of utter release the sight inspired.

Spending time with Kyle this evening hadn't felt like work, it hadn't felt like a challenge, it had merely felt right.

She shook herself back to reality and hugged herself.

"Cold?" Kyle asked.

Sara started to answer that she was fine, but then realized a fabricated need for her jacket or a sweater would give her the opportunity to slip back into Kyle's home unaccompanied.

"A little." She nodded. "I'll just run in and get my jacket."

"Perfect. I'll get things warmed up out here," Kyle said as he headed toward a large stone fire pit.

Sara stood still momentarily, watching the ease with which the man moved. The confidence he showed in every step he took. She realized then that she didn't want him to be the brains behind the TCM conspiracy.

She wanted him to be innocent, wanted him to be an unknowing pawn in someone else's game.

But Kyle Prescott didn't strike her as the kind of man who would be a pawn in anyone's game.

Evangeline had been right.

Her stepson's legendary charm had wreaked havoc with Sara's objectivity.

"I'll be right back," she said as she turned, headed back toward the house.

She needed to shove all thoughts of Kyle's guilt or innocence out of her mind and focus on one thing. Accessing the evidence she needed as quickly as possible.

If Kyle were innocent, the evidence would support the truth.

If he were guilty...

If he were guilty, Sara would do what she'd done in every case before this one.

She'd turn in her man.

No matter how deeply this one had gotten beneath her skin.

She grabbed her jacket from where Kyle had hung it in the hall closet and slipped it over her shoulders as she headed for his office.

There wasn't a moment to spare.

Starting the fire might keep Kyle occupied for a few minutes, but not much more. If she were lucky, his computer would be on stand-by as it had been the night before.

The moment she stepped into his office she realized she was out of luck.

Not only was the screen black, but the monitor's power indicator was dark as well. The system was off.

Sara stole a glance at the hallway then sighed inwardly.

There wasn't time to power on the system and dig.

Damn.

She'd have to find another way.

A notepad sat to the side of Kyle's monitor and she squinted in the dark to make out his handwriting.

Kingston Trust.

Land assessments.

Agreements of sale.

Land coordinates.

Sara's pulse quickened, her heart beginning a steady drumming against her ribs.

If only she could copy this sheet, or commit every word to memory, but there wasn't time.

She took a quick inventory of Kyle's office equipment, but saw no copier. No fax machine. No visible sign of anything that would allow her to copy his notes.

What had he been doing? Making note of documents he'd uncovered? Or keeping track of evidence he needed to destroy?

Sara ran her finger down the list, groaning with disappointment when she found not a single investor name. She mentally berated herself. She knew better than to think she'd unlock the mystery of Kingston Trust so easily.

"Damn," she muttered under her breath, just as Kyle's voice sounded from the doorway.

"Don't even try to tell me you wanted to admire the view." All sign of affection had left his tone, his voice now serious and curt. "That one's not going to work again. Not this time."

Sara stared into his level gaze. What was she going

to tell him? The truth? That she'd been desperately trying to figure out a way to lift or copy his notes?

She needed to come up with something before he suspected the reason for tonight's visit had been anything other than an innocent food delivery.

Truth was she'd intended to find evidence to point the finger of guilt at TCM.

She traced her fingertip down the tablet.

She'd not only found evidence to implicate TCM, but apparently Kyle, as well.

"Sara?"

"Sorry." She shook herself out of her trance, her brain racing through possible answers to Kyle's question when she struck on genius. "I wanted to leave you a thank-you note."

She offered an innocent shrug, spinning her deception even as Kyle's gaze grew more suspicious. "I thought if I left it here you'd find it sometime tomorrow. A surprise."

Sara forced herself to stop talking. She had more sense than to babble under pressure.

The trick now would be to lock stares with Kyle until he was the first to speak.

But before either of them could say a word or make a move, voices sounded from outside Kyle's home.

Loud voices.

Angry voices.

"What in the—"

Kyle stalked down the hall toward the front door,

seemingly forgetting about his interrogation of Sara's true motivation. He'd no sooner wrenched open the front door than Sara heard a series of pops.

Loud. Life-threatening.

Gunfire.

"Kyle!"

She launched herself at him, slamming her full weight into his chest, taking him down to the hardwood in a split second.

Sara searched Kyle's stunned expression, surprised by the anxiety firing through her system. Had he been hurt?

"I'm fine." Kyle extricated himself from beneath her, grasping both of her elbows as he slid her to one side. "I need to make sure no one's been hurt."

"You need to call the police," she answered, reaching reflexively for her ankle weapon but remembering it sat safely tucked away in her glove compartment.

The precaution had no doubt been for the best, or else she'd be sitting here now trying to explain the pistol in her boot to Kyle.

He scrambled to his feet. "We don't have time for the police."

The unmistakable sound of retreating footsteps filled the otherwise quiet night air.

Sara pulled herself up from the floor, moving close behind him as he raced out the front door.

Kyle spun on her, protectiveness blatant in his gaze. "Stay put."

Stay put?

She'd never stayed put a day in her life and she wasn't about to start now. Socialite cover, or not.

Kyle raced ahead, down his driveway toward the street.

A dark object slumped in a heap, unmistakably out of place on the dirt shoulder across the street.

Sara followed, close on Kyle's heels, wishing fervently she had her weapon. Rushing unarmed into the pitch-black Colorado night with a gunman on the loose was not the brightest thing either of them had ever done.

Yet someone had been wounded, and perhaps lay dying just yards away. They had no choice but to rush forward.

Kyle reached the body first, dropping to his knees as he skidded to a stop. He pressed his fingers to the man's neck just as Sara kneeled beside him, taking in the features of the downed man.

His salt-and-pepper hair appeared to be expertly trimmed and the fabric and cut of his shirt suggested money. Lots of money.

Kyle sucked in a sharp breath. "I can't find a pulse."

Sara's focus fell to the bullet hole in the man's chest. In the center of his heart. The small circumference of blood around the bullet hole suggested his heart had stopped pumping almost instantaneously.

She winced.

"I don't think you're going to find a pulse."

She pointed to the wound and Kyle followed her gesture, grimacing at the sight of the mortal wound.

"Who is he?" Sara asked.

Kyle shook his head. "I've never seen him before."

Without thinking, Sara expertly searched the man's pockets for any sign of identification, but came up empty-handed.

Kyle was already on his feet, peering into the dark night.

"You'll never find anyone now," Sara said, reading his mind. "Whoever did this is long gone."

"But it's only been a matter of minutes."

She looked up at him, felt her insides twist at the genuine tension painted across his face. "That's all it takes, Kyle. He's gone."

Kyle squinted and shook his head. "You go back to the house, I have to try."

He took off in a sprint, not waiting for her response.

This time, Sara made a quick pit stop at her car before she followed. If the shooter was still out there somewhere she'd be damned if she was going to rush in unarmed.

Based on Kyle's expression and sincere reaction to tonight's events, he'd been bumped from the top of her suspect list.

But could he still somehow be involved? Responsible?

Had tonight been an act? Orchestrated for her benefit?

She drew in a deep breath as she gripped her gun and set off after Kyle.

She wasn't sure of anything at the moment but one thing. No matter what Kyle's role was—or had been—in the murder-for-oil conspiracy, she planned to keep him alive until she got her answers.

After all, she was only doing her job.

The sharp twist of her stomach belied her thoughts. She could argue with herself all she wanted to about objectivity, but the reality was her thoughts on Kyle Prescott had become subjective.

She'd always been a big believer in gut instinct combined with good old-fashioned investigative work. The problem in this case was that her gut didn't believe Kyle capable of the crime, while the evidence indicated anything but.

Sara refocused, listening for footfalls. Surprise slid through her when she heard none.

Damn.

She should have risked the pursuit unarmed. Now that she'd lost Kyle, her weapon wouldn't do him a bit of good if needed.

Someone moved off to her right and she spun on one heel, leveling her pistol at the noise.

Kyle emerged from the foliage, eyes wide with adrenaline and surprise. He pointed at Sara's gun. "A little something you picked up at finishing school?"

She shook her head, lowering her weapon. "I'm a self-defense advocate."

Kyle rubbed his shoulder as he headed past her back toward where the victim's body had fallen. "I guess that explains the cracked shoulder you gave me when you body-slammed me."

"I thought someone was shooting at you," she explained, quickening her pace to catch up to him.

"Pardon me for saying this—" Kyle slowed long enough to pin her with a sharp look "—but you are unlike any other woman I've ever met."

"I'll take that as a compliment."

"I'm not entirely sure you should."

Sara glared at his back as he turned away, frowning when he came to a sudden stop, looking first in one direction and then the other.

"Did you move him?" He pivoted to face her.

Sara's brows snapped together. "What are you talking about?"

Kyle gestured widely. "You tell me."

The body was gone. Not a shred of evidence remained where the man had been.

No clothing.

No blood.

Nothing except for visible signs of trampled foliage and dirt—most from Kyle and Sara, no doubt.

Kyle lifted his puzzled gaze to Sara, and they stood in dumbfounded silence.

If she didn't know better, Sara would swear they'd imagined the entire thing.

Chapter Eight

Kyle shoved a hand through his hair and longingly envisioned a glass of scotch.

He and Sara had searched his entire property from road to garage to pasture and back again.

They'd found nothing.

No trace of the shooter, and certainly no trace of the victim.

If he didn't know better, he'd swear they'd both hallucinated the entire event.

Sara blinked then shook her head. "We've got to be looking in the wrong spot."

They stood on the precise spot where the body had fallen. Sara searched the area, frantically pacing in a wider and wider arc.

Kyle stepped close, grasping her elbows. He gave her a quick shake and Sara's dazed look locked with his.

Energy spiked between them, fueled by the emotions of the evening and the anxiety of not knowing who had been behind the shooting or the disappearing body.

"I know my land," he said flatly. "The body's gone. Someone took it." He tipped his chin toward her car, less than fifty yards away. "Someone took it while you were right there retrieving your gun."

"Surely you don't think I had something to do with this?" Indignation fired in her gaze and she jerked her arms free of his touch. "Maybe you set this whole thing up. Maybe the body wasn't dead to begin with."

Kyle pressed his lips into a thin line then gave a tight nod. "You're right. We could both be lying, but I have a feeling we're not. Someone out there wanted whoever that was dead, and didn't care that we saw. That tells me whoever it was won't hesitate to shut us up if needed."

They both fell silent.

This time when Kyle reached for her, Sara didn't resist, instead she slid her slender hand into his as they headed back toward the house.

"Shall I call the police?" she asked as they neared the front steps.

Kyle gave her hand a sharp squeeze. "No police."

Sara's expression morphed from one of total shock to one of total disbelief. "We have to report this."

"Report what?" He leaned so close he could feel her breath on his face. "No body? No gun? No shooter?"

Kyle stepped past her to push the door open, fatigue sliding into the spaces his fading adrenaline had left behind.

"They'll either think we're insane," he continued, "or they'll speculate we're covering something up." He rubbed his face as he headed toward the kitchen. "I'd rather not add to my troubles right now."

Sara's tone intensified, going sharp. "What troubles?"

Damn. He'd said too much.

"Nothing," he answered. "Just a few things at work."

Like a huge land acquisition project, bearing my signature, of which I knew nothing.

"Scotch?"

"No, thanks." Sara stepped into the kitchen behind him, leaning against the granite-topped island. Her cheeks were flushed a bright pink, no doubt from the combination of chilly night air and excitement. "I'd probably better get going."

"No." Kyle shook his head and took a long swallow of the scotch he'd poured. He moaned as the hot liquid spread over his tongue and down his throat. The numbing heat was exactly what he needed. "Whoever was here tonight may very well have seen us, whereas we saw nothing."

"We saw the body," she interjected.

Kyle nodded. "My point is that if the shooter saw you, you might be at a distinct disadvantage out there alone tonight. I'd like you to stay here."

He hadn't known he was going to issue the invitation until the words slipped from his mouth.

Kyle knew he'd been overcome with an odd sense of protectiveness the moment the shots rang out. His first thought had been of Sara's safety. Her welfare had remained front and center in his thoughts ever since.

"I'd feel better if you stayed in one of the guest rooms. I need to know you're safe tonight and the only way I can do that is to keep you here."

Sara opened her mouth, apparently ready to protest, but quickly snapped it shut.

"All right. Thank you."

Kyle paused for a split second, surprise at her lack of argument washing through him. "Excellent." He tipped his head toward the hall. "You'll find each bedroom fully equipped with toiletries, bathrobes, anything you might need."

Their eyes locked for a long moment before Sara turned to walk away.

"Is there anything else you think you'll require?" he asked, as he hoisted his glass of scotch to his lips once more.

Sara shook her head as she walked out of the kitchen toward the bedrooms. "I think I've had just about everything I can handle for one night."

Kyle sat pondering her comment as he listened to her footsteps fade.

The woman was more resilient than anyone he'd

ever met, certainly more than the other women who had passed in and out of his life.

Most women—hell, most men—would have gone squeamish at the sight of a dead body and the prospect of chasing a shooter into the dark Colorado night. Sara, on the other hand, hadn't hesitated for a moment.

Matter of fact, she'd retrieved her *weapon* and jumped right in.

He drained the last of the scotch from the glass and reached for the bottle. He let his hand fall before he made contact.

The last thing he needed right now was more alcohol.

He needed to get back into the TCM system and print hard copies of everything he'd found. Computer log be damned.

He'd planned to make contact with Powers tonight, but that hadn't worked out. He'd do so first thing in the morning. He couldn't let whatever it was Powers had contacted him about hang out in the unknown anymore.

The time had come to face the man, but Kyle planned to be fully prepared when he did so.

He made his way toward the hallway, pausing outside the one closed bedroom door.

Sara had chosen the room farthest from his master suite. Why? Because she didn't trust herself to be any closer? Or because she wanted as much space between them as possible?

Kyle's gut caught and twisted.

The sexual tension between the two of them had begun to grow, there was no doubt about it. The question was what was fueling that tension. Genuine attraction?

Or had the events of the past few days taken control of their thoughts and actions?

Kyle listened outside the bedroom door, hearing nothing. He continued past, fighting the urge to step inside to see if Sara felt the same physical need he'd begun to experience.

He shoved that thought out of his mind and stepped into his office, instantly remembering the sight of Sara at his desk, supposedly leaving him a note.

He'd forgotten all about the encounter once the shots rang out. No surprise there.

But what had she been doing?

Leaving a note as she claimed? Or nosing around in his personal affairs?

Kyle took a quick inventory of his desk and found everything as he'd left it, right down to the series of numbers he'd jotted down from the electronic records he'd discovered last night.

He powered on his computer system and sank into his chair, kicking his feet up onto his desk and turning to take in the expansive view outside the room.

Colorado never ceased to amaze him.

So much land.

So much sky.

So many hidden treasures…and secrets.

Once the start screen displayed on his monitor, Kyle dropped his feet to the floor and his focus to the task at hand. He worked deftly, gaining access into the TCM virtual network with no difficulty.

Yet this time when he pulled up the folder containing the Kingston welcome memos, he blinked.

The list of files was far shorter than he remembered.

He clicked on the first file name but received nothing but an error message.

File not found.

He clicked on the next file in the list.

File not found.

"Son of a—"

He backed out of the folder then reselected it, hoping the system's failure to open the files had been a fluke, only this time the sight that greeted him left him cold.

The list of files was gone. Vanished right before his eyes.

Someone must be in the system at the same time, clearing out the evidence.

But who? Johnson?

Kyle snapped the phone on his desk from its base and pressed the speed-dial button for the building. The answering service picked up after just a few rings. Kyle didn't wait to exchange pleasantries.

"This is Kyle Prescott. Patch me through to the guard on duty. Immediately."

"Yes, sir."

A sleepy male voice came on the line in a matter of seconds. "Yes, Mr. Prescott."

"Has anyone checked into the building tonight after hours?"

"No, sir." The note of surprise in the guard's voice was unmistakable.

"How about someone working late?"

"No, sir. Last time I made my rounds, I checked each office. Everyone's gone, Mr. Prescott."

"Thank you."

Kyle disconnected the call and blew out a frustrated breath. Apparently he wasn't the only one savvy enough to tap into the network from a remote location.

He refocused on the notes on his desk and the list of files and folders he'd discovered the night before.

He worked to open folder after folder, document after document, meeting with the same result each time.

They were gone.

Every document detailing land assessments and purchases was gone…at least in electronic form.

Someone had deleted every shred of evidence faster than Kyle could open the files.

But who? And why now?

Was tonight's shooter somehow connected to whatever it was that was going on?

Kyle pushed back from the desk and walked toward the wall. He leaned heavily against the glass, staring out into the darkness, wondering what and whom he was up against.

And what about the woman sleeping in the guest room down the hall?

Was she somehow connected to the events of the past three days?

He powered off his computer then flicked off the office light, turning not toward his suite, but rather back toward the kitchen and the bottle of scotch.

He'd suddenly grown tired of the questions haunting him. Right now he didn't want to give another thought to the missing files, and he didn't want to give a second thought to Sara. In his home. Under his roof.

He was beginning to feel too much for the woman and right now he didn't want to feel anything.

Not anything at all.

WHEN KYLE HANDED Sara the perfect excuse to remain close to his office and computer, she hadn't hesitated.

He'd no doubt thought her quick agreement to be nothing other than a choice made by a fragile female in need of protection. Little did he know she'd already filed a report with headquarters and now waited only for the man to go to bed.

When the house fell silent, she quietly made her way toward his office, barefoot. She frowned at the soft glow of light spilling from the partially open office door.

The unmistakable sound of fingers on a keyboard filtered into the hall.

Damn.

Just when she thought she'd have all the time in the world to access the TCM system and make some sense of the notes she'd found scribbled all over the tablet on his desk.

Not wanting to give herself away, she dropped to her knees and crawled toward the door, positioning herself to be able to see Kyle's desk through the open crack, remembering that the computer chair faced away from the door.

As she watched, he swore loudly, then snatched up the office phone. His words were unmistakable. He had reason to suspect someone was inside the TCM building.

But why? And why would the possibility leave him so visibly upset?

Then it hit her.

Something had changed with the files, or with his ability to access the files.

Sara bit back a groan.

She had to get inside that system before any possible evidence was altered or destroyed.

When Kyle pushed away from the desk and headed toward the window, Sara backtracked toward her room.

She couldn't risk getting caught. Not after the little episode earlier when she'd told him she was in his office to leave him a note.

She rolled her eyes. Pathetic excuse, yet one he seemed to have believed.

Sara had no sooner eased her bedroom door shut than she heard Kyle's footsteps in the hall, headed not toward his master suite but rather back toward the home's living area.

No matter.

If there was one thing she'd learned in her line of work, it was patience. If she had to wait all night for the chance to access Kyle's computer system, she would.

When Kyle's footsteps sounded again, this time headed back toward his sleeping area, her heartbeat picked up a notch.

Finally.

She'd give him fifteen minutes then she'd go back to his office. This time, she was going to uncover exactly what the man had been up to.

When she headed back out into the hall, she smiled at the sight of nothing but darkness coming from the space at the bottom of Kyle's bedroom door.

She flashed on the image of the man in bed, probably shirtless, hunkered down beneath expensive sheets. Her mouth went dry and her insides warmed.

No, she mentally chided herself.

No matter what she'd begun to feel for Kyle, she needed to ignore it. She *had* to ignore it.

Sara stepped into the office, easing the door shut behind her. She found the system's power switch by equal parts memory and touch, and waited until the monitor cast enough light for her to operate.

She retraced her steps from the other night, frowning when she pulled up the Kingston folder.

Nothing. None of the welcome memos she'd spotted existed—not anymore.

Maybe Kyle had checked on whether or not someone was at TCM headquarters because he didn't want to get caught deleting files.

Did he really think he could get away with it?

Regret filtered through her.

Had Kyle masterminded the entire investment and murder scheme? Her training and the evidence she'd gathered so far told her he very well might have, but her gut and her heart protested otherwise.

Damn.

She'd spent her entire adult life focusing on her career and avoiding personal entanglements for just this reason.

Emotions made you weak. Plain and simple.

Sara traced a finger over the mess of notations Kyle had made on the notepad.

A series of numbers and document names. If she weren't mistaken, the numbers were formatted in the same pattern as the land coordinates that had been sent to TCM headquarters.

Once more she scanned Kyle's office for any sign of a machine capable of copying the paper.

She found none.

Sara hesitated for only a few seconds before she carefully removed the sheet of paper from the tablet.

As she saw it, she had no other choice.

Someone else had died tonight, no doubt somehow connected to the oil conspiracy. She needed hard proof of TCM's involvement and she needed it now. If she had to blow her cover in order to expose the guilty parties, so be it.

She folded the paper in half and then in half again, tucking it into the pocket of her jeans.

She powered off the computer and waited for the screen to go black.

This time when she stepped back into the hall, she stopped in the guest room just long enough to retrieve her boots. She planned to be long gone before Kyle noticed her missing, and hopefully by then she'd have figured out exactly what the notations on the paper had to do with the case.

As she eased the door shut behind her and headed for her car, she did her best to ignore the one thought tapping at the base of her brain.

The puzzle pieces seemed to be coming together, but what would she do if they pointed the finger of guilt directly at one person?

Kyle Prescott.

WHEN THE DOORBELL woke Kyle the next morning it took him a few seconds to place the noise.

He rolled over in bed, wincing at the bright sunlight easing around the edges of the bedroom drapes. What time was it?

He tried to swallow, doing his best to pry his tongue from the roof of his mouth.

He glanced at the empty glass on his nightstand and remembered. Scotch.

He'd been drinking scotch.

Far too much, apparently.

Kyle pulled a sweatshirt over his head just as the doorbell chimed again, this time accompanied by a series of knocks. He stepped into a pair of jeans and headed toward the hall.

"Just a minute."

He paused just long enough at the guest room door where Sara had slept to realize she hadn't slept at all. The room looked completely untouched.

He frowned, wondering why she'd changed her mind.

When he pulled open the front door, all thoughts of Sara Montgomery and her sleeping habits fled his mind.

Two men in suits stood on his front step, their faces set in matching serious expressions, their hair cut in matching close-cropped styles.

"Can I help you?" Kyle reached up to smooth the hair he realized hadn't been touched since he'd rolled out of bed.

"Mr. Kyle Prescott?" the larger of the two men asked.

Kyle nodded.

"Denver police, Mr. Prescott. We need to ask you a few questions."

After the murder he'd witnessed the night before, Kyle wasn't about to believe anything anyone had to say.

"I'd like to see some identification."

"Understandable." The larger man flipped open his ID. "Senior Detective Norris." He gestured toward the smaller man who also extended his badge. "Detective Winston."

Kyle took a long moment to scrutinize both badges even though he had no idea how to spot a fake if indeed these weren't genuine. The sinking feeling in his stomach, however, told him these were the real deal.

And if two Denver detectives had shown up at his front door first thing this morning, it could only mean one thing.

Sara had reported the shooting and phantom body even after he'd told her not to.

"Is this about last night?" Kyle asked the question hoping to be proactive. His plan backfired instantly.

"So you're not denying your involvement?" the shorter man, Winston, asked.

"Involvement?" Kyle frowned.

"In the shooting, sir."

"I heard the shooting and saw the body before it disappeared, but I'd hardly say I was involved."

The two men exchanged a glance that set Kyle's teeth on edge.

"Did you know the victim, sir?"

Kyle furrowed his brow. "I'd never seen the man before."

"Jonathan Powers, sir?"

The bottom fell out of Kyle's stomach. "Jonathan Powers?"

"His wife last saw him when he left to meet with you. What can you tell us about that?"

Kyle blinked. "Nothing. I had no meeting planned with this man."

"But you did know him?"

"No," Kyle answered quickly, probably too quickly. "I'd received a call from him, but I didn't know him."

"What kind of call?"

That he had proof of my signature on documentation damaging to TCM.

Kyle could just imagine what would happen next if he delivered that line. Instead he gave a quick shrug. "An inquiry about TCM."

Detective Norris pointed to the home's foyer. "May we come in, Mr. Prescott?"

"Of course." Kyle stepped to one side, taking note of the way the men scanned every inch of the visible interior in the few seconds it took them to step inside.

"Have you found the body?" he asked.

Senior Detective Norris widened his eyes. "We suspect you already know the answer to that question."

Kyle scrubbed a hand across the stubble on his chin, wondering for a split second just how ragged he looked. "I told you. The body disappeared."

"The body didn't disappear, sir," Winston said.

Kyle frowned at the man. "Then where is it?"

"Mr. Powers's body was found by your garage, Mr. Prescott, next to the remains of a motorcycle registered in your name."

Kyle's head spun. Next to the garage? There had been no body there last night. No body anywhere on his land.

"Did someone find it?" he asked.

"We did, sir. When we followed up on Mrs. Powers's lead that her husband was to meet with you."

Kyle wanted to confirm Sara had nothing to do with this, but he didn't want to drop her name into the conversation. She had nothing to do with any of this mess, and if there were any way possible to keep her out of the investigation, Kyle would do so.

"I suppose you'd like me to go with you now?" Kyle asked.

Norris nodded, his features tense.

"Let me grab something from my office, and splash some water on my face, if you don't mind."

"Winston will accompany you," Norris said. "I'm sure you understand."

Kyle nodded, but he in no way understood.

He'd gone to bed stunned over the fact someone had been murdered on his property and then vanished.

He'd apparently woken up this morning as a suspect—a suspect the Denver police didn't trust to so much as brush his teeth without escaping.

He headed toward his office, the smaller detective on his heels. Once there, he grabbed his BlackBerry from the drawer, having a sinking suspicion he'd need access to his numbers.

When his gaze dropped to the tablet he'd left on his desk, his throat constricted.

Blank.

His notes gone.

Only one person would have had access to this room, and he'd thought she'd been asleep when he was in here working last night.

Sara.

Had she set him up?

Kyle steeled himself, suddenly furious at everything that had happened.

The stolen signature.

The forged documents.

The body dumped on his land.

Determination welled in his chest and he spun on Winston. "I have nothing to hide. I didn't shoot that man, and I have no idea of who did."

"Evidence says different, Mr. Prescott." The detective jerked his thumb back toward the foyer. "I need you to hurry it up. We're going to need you to take a ride."

Chapter Nine

Kyle stared in disbelief at the group gathered inside the police station upon his arrival. He'd continued to weigh the possibility of Sara's involvement on the ride over, but his gut refused to believe it.

The fact that she'd disappeared overnight—apparently with his notes—while the body had reappeared was nothing more than a coincidence.

It had to be.

When Kyle stepped into an interrogation room and spotted Evangeline Prescott leaning her hip against the table, dread and curiosity fired inside him. What on earth was she doing here?

He then turned to the woman next to her.

Sara.

So his gut had been wrong.

Very wrong.

Kyle studied the tense expression on Sara's face, the hint of anxiousness in her eyes. He'd never seen anyone look more guilty.

"Why?" Kyle pinned Sara with a glare.

She said nothing, her throat working.

"There's a simple explanation." Evangeline moved to step forward, but Sara placed her hand on the other woman's elbow, stopping her short.

"I'll take care of this."

Kyle barely recognized Sara's voice. Her tone had gone emotionless. Flat.

She crossed quickly to where he stood, meeting his questioning glare head-on. She hesitated before she spoke, narrowed her eyes, then began.

"I'm an investigator for Prescott Personal Securities."

Kyle let loose with a string of expletives. He'd never so much as asked the woman what she did for a living and she certainly hadn't offered.

What a fool he'd been.

"I was charged with infiltrating TCM to get to the bottom of the Kingston Trust investor deaths."

So their time together had been nothing more than a ruse. Nothing more than an act to gain access to his family's firm.

"And I was the handy lackey you decided to use?" He straightened, determined not to let his body language convey one ounce of the sense of betrayal surging through his veins.

Sara winced, and Kyle took some small satisfaction at the sight. He'd hit a nerve, not an easy feat when it came to Ms. Montgomery.

She said nothing to Kyle, but rather turned to Detective Norris.

"I can vouch for this man." Her words rang confident and believable. "I was with him at the time of the shooting and I witnessed the body's disappearance just as he did."

"And the fingerprints on the gun?" The detective's eyebrows lifted toward his hairline.

"Someone's setting Mr. Prescott up for a fall," Sara answered. "I have reason to believe documents have been forged under his signature and now someone has planted the evidence in an attempt to pin this murder on him as well."

Kyle stood in stunned silence.

Sara Montgomery was obviously very good at her job. He'd said nothing in her presence to let her know about the documents, yet she knew. She'd obviously bugged his office somehow or hacked into his computer.

Realization hit him.

He'd been right when he'd thought she might not be popping into his office for the view.

The betrayal lingering inside him gave way to a mix of anger and gratitude.

Anger that he'd allowed himself to be so thoroughly used by the woman, and gratitude that she'd provided him with an alibi.

When Evangeline spoke, her crisp voice sent a chill racing down Kyle's back.

"You're to be released into our custody, Kyle." She paused dramatically. "Prescott Personal Securities. If Sara says you're innocent, you're innocent."

"We, however—" Detective Norris leaned close "—will believe you're innocent when someone proves to us the evidence is fake."

"We'll do just that, Detective." Evangeline reached for Kyle's arm but he moved clear of her touch.

"I'll drive him." Sara stepped into the small group, directing her words toward Evangeline and not toward him.

"I'm right here," he said. "You may view me as nothing more than an object in your investigation, but I'd prefer to be addressed when you're talking about me."

Sara gave a quick shake of her head and set off toward the exit door. "Hurry up, then."

Kyle took her move as his cue to get the hell out of the police station. He followed her into the cool late morning air, his anger ready to explode.

He didn't say a word, choosing instead to wait until they were inside Sara's car and on the road.

He planned to make sure Sara Montgomery was a captive audience when he launched his interrogation.

BLATANT FURY PULSATED inside Kyle.

He'd been blindsided. And Sara had been the one to do the dirty work.

"Nice job." He spoke the words coolly, obviously working to avoid injecting his anger into his words.

"I know you're upset right now." Sara leveled her eyes at him quickly then refocused on the road as they headed into downtown Denver. "But I'm on your side."

"Really?" His anger had moved from a boil to a full-out roll. "Because, correct me if I'm wrong, but you were standing on the other side of the room back there."

"Only to explain things."

"Then start explaining."

"There have been a series of recent deaths. All wealthy business owners or CEOs. All who either personally, or through their corporations, owned large parcels of oil-rich land."

Kyle frowned, concentrating on the implication of Sara's words.

"All murdered after they'd made an investment or had sold out to Kingston Trust."

"Operated by Kingston Investments," Kyle said flatly. "And all welcomed into the fold by me personally." He shook his head. "Or at least someone sharp enough to steal my electronic signature."

Sara nodded. "Exactly."

Silence beat between them.

"There's more." Sara's words jerked Kyle's attention away from the mental images of dead investors. Had Johnson masterminded the entire conspiracy? It didn't seem possible.

"Your initials were found in two of the dead men's notebooks. Jonathan Powers being the most recent."

"Powers had contacted me."

Kyle took some small satisfaction in the surprise that flashed across Sara's refined features. At least he had known one thing she hadn't yet uncovered.

"He left a voice mail the day I first met you. The thought you might be involved had actually crossed my mind." He shook his head. "I never thought you were on the other side, trying to pin me for a crime."

"I'm not trying to pin you for a crime." Sara's voice climbed in intensity.

"Then what are you trying to do?"

"I'm trying to stop whoever is behind this before anyone else—like Jonathan Powers—gets killed."

"Is that why you stole my notes?"

She grew silent again momentarily then continued. "Yes." She plunged ahead as if that particular part of the conversation was closed. "Why did Powers call you?"

Kyle squeezed his eyes shut and tipped his head back against the seat. "That's what I was trying to find out."

"He was next on the list."

"The list?" Kyle snapped his head forward, turning to study Sara's every expression.

"A coded list of land coordinates." She paused as she maneuvered the car into an underground parking area, amazingly well-hidden from the center city street.

"A disk was anonymously sent to our offices," Sara continued. "We haven't yet been able to extract any names from the list. Only land coordinates."

"Connected to the murders?"

"Now that we have more evidence? Yes. A perfect match."

Kyle swore loudly. "And someone at TCM is behind this?"

"Someone's pulling the strings under the guise of Kingston Trust."

"And using my name to do it."

Sara nodded. "Your signature has been used on every land acquisition file we've found connected to Kingston. You're the perfect patsy." Sara slid the car into a parking space and cut the engine. "You have to admit that."

Kyle rankled, but silently admitted she was correct. "I'm never in the office, yet I'm high-ranking enough to have the power to pull something like this off."

Sara reached for the door, but Kyle gripped her arm. Her pale gaze lifted to his, searching his face.

"One more thing." Kyle leaned closer to the driver's seat.

Sara stilled and their gazes locked.

"Our day together at Red Rocks? The call from my stepmother? Your polite and caring questions about whether or not she and I were close? About my family? My father...? All an act?"

Sara grimaced. "I had a job to do."

Kyle did his best to shove down the unfamiliar sense of disappointment that slid through his system. "Fair enough. I just wanted to know what I was dealing with."

She smiled, the look in sharp contrast to the deadly conspiracy she'd just described and the tension hanging heavy inside the car. "I'm not sorry for what I did. I've learned enough to believe you innocent. Now you and I just have to prove it."

SARA WALKED AHEAD of Kyle, not allowing the man to catch up, not that she was actually sure he'd try. She knew he'd follow her. What other choice did he have? He'd been released into her custody and that of PPS.

Without their cooperation, he was headed straight for a Denver holding cell while the local police compiled their list of circumstantial evidence against him.

Kyle didn't say a word as he stepped into the elevator behind her. The two turned to face the front, both pairs of eyes locked on the numbered display above the door.

At the top floor, Sara stepped off before giving Kyle a chance to move. She crossed to the PPS security screen and allowed the sensor to scan her irises.

The doors slid open and she stepped across the threshold. She turned to tell Kyle to follow, but he was so close on her heels he bumped her as they passed through.

Angel sat at the reception desk, her expression a mixture of curiosity and restraint.

Sara knew for a fact Evangeline had been schooling Angel on the proper reactions during times like these, but Sara had yet to see the fruit of Evangeline's efforts. She realized she might have been wrong in her assessment of Angel's ability to conform.

"Angel."

"Sara."

"Good to see you, Angel." The sound of Kyle's voice took Sara by surprise. "You're looking striking, as usual," he continued.

Sara frowned momentarily, then realized Kyle had no doubt been to the office at some point. She shouldn't be surprised he was on a first-name basis with Angel, but she was.

His world and Sara's world couldn't be farther apart yet here he was blending seamlessly into the world she'd thought miles above his world, ethically, when she'd first met him.

Kyle represented everything she'd grown to hate during her life. Yet the few days she'd known him had shown the man to be far more than a rich playboy working at the family conglomerate.

Kyle Prescott had shown her his soft side, a genuine warmth she was fairly confident he didn't let most of his romantic conquests witness.

Kyle Prescott had shown her his heart, and that had been something Sara had never expected the man to possess, let alone demonstrate.

"Evangeline's waiting for you," Angel said. "It's good to see you again, Mr. Prescott."

"Kyle," he answered. As he and Sara headed toward Evangeline's corner office, he dropped his voice low. "How'd she beat us here? Broom?"

Sara acknowledged the disrespectful comment with a glare.

"Not all of us hold your mighty leader in such high esteem, Ms. Montgomery."

Sara bristled. "Well, I do. I find her nothing but admirable."

"Well, then," Kyle said as he pushed open the door to Evangeline's office without knocking, "that makes one of us."

Evangeline barely looked up from her desk when they entered. Not a sleek blond hair fell out of place, and her impeccable gray suit showed no sign she'd recently been in the midst of the precinct's chaotic environment, waiting for her stepson to be brought in on suspicion of murder.

She glanced quickly at Sara, her eyes narrowing as if she sensed Kyle had gotten under Sara's skin. Evangeline then lifted a manila envelope, thrusting it in Kyle's direction.

"This is everything we have on you thus far. Sara's already been briefed. Should you have any questions at all, she's the person to ask." Evangeline tipped her head to one side and studied Kyle momentarily. "Sara feels very strongly that you're innocent. For the sake of your father's memory, I hope she's correct."

Kyle took the offered envelope but said nothing, and merely glared at Evangeline.

"I trust you'll use that information to plan the best way to access TCM records," Evangeline continued.

"What if they're already destroyed?"

Evangeline's perfect lips pressed into a tight line. "Then you, my dear boy, are in a world of trouble." She returned her focus to the work spread across her desktop. "Keep me posted."

"Always," Sara replied as she turned to leave.

Kyle had already cleared the door and stepped into the hall. He spun on Sara as soon as she'd crossed the office's threshold.

"If you think I'm going to take marching orders from her—" he jerked his thumb toward Evangeline's office "—or you, you're sadly mistaken."

Sara grasped his elbow and dragged him away from Evangeline's office. "Not here."

To her surprise, Kyle put up no struggle, following her as she approached the ladies room door.

"This is one of two spots inside PPS offices without surveillance."

Kyle said nothing, but the raw fury blatant in his gaze spoke volumes. "Big stepmother is watching?"

His arrogant tone made the small hairs at the base of Sara's neck stand at attention.

At that moment, she saw the Kyle Prescott she'd

always heard about. Cocky. Wise-ass. Emotionally distant.

She knew better than to fall for the tough facade. She wasn't about to let him shut her out now. Not when they were this close to blowing the TCM conspiracy wide open.

Sara needed Kyle to be helpful and accommodating, and to do that she had to slap off the chip that had appeared on his shoulder.

She tightened her grip and pulled him toward the bathroom stalls, each one looking more like a small apartment than a restroom.

"Are you sure they aren't using potty cams?" Kyle jerked his arm free of her touch.

"Quite sure." Sara's frustration with the man had shifted from a simmer to a boil. "You'd better listen to me, Kyle, and then you'd better get over yourself."

"And what if I don't?"

"Then you'll be going to jail for a very long time." She reached out and touched the stubble along his jaw, her belly tightening with the contact.

She moved to lower her hand. "I'm not sure you'll be able to keep up the casually unkempt look on the inside that you've so carefully perfected on the outside."

Kyle gripped her wrist. "If that's all you think I'm about, then you can take your little investigation and shove it right up your—"

"That attitude's not going to get you very far," Sara interrupted, leveling her gaze at him.

He pulled her closer and lowered his voice. "It was working just fine before you came along."

Sara straightened to meet his stare. "Could have fooled—"

His lips were on hers before she could finish her sentence. She tensed, then relaxed into him as his arms slid around her waist, pressing into the small of her back and pulling her body flush against his.

Heat exploded inside her, the intensity of her desire shoving aside all of the anger and frustration she'd been feeling just a split second before.

Kyle's lips pressed hers apart and his tongue tangled with hers for several mind-numbing seconds before she regained her senses and pushed away from him, breaking all contact.

"What's the matter? Your debutante training kick in?" Kyle's voice had gone thick, but his cold features showed no sign of the heat that had just passed between them.

Sara swallowed down her frustration and steeled herself. "What if it did?"

The corner of his mouth pulled into a smug grin. "Then you're no better than I am, babe."

Babe.

The word made her skin crawl, but she kept her focus on what really mattered.

Assuring Kyle's cooperation. Apparently, he'd already made up his mind.

Kyle headed toward the door, pausing with his

hand on the handle. "Report to the office at eight tomorrow. Sharp." He looked back at her, his features set, the line of his jaw firm. "You'll be the company's new image consultant. Do you think you're capable of pulling that off?"

"I fooled you, didn't I?"

His expression turned lethal. "Trust me. That won't happen again."

Then he pushed through the exit door and was gone.

Chapter Ten

Sara didn't wait for an invitation to come in when Kyle opened the door. Instead, she slung her overnight bag over her shoulder and pushed past him.

Evangeline had cornered her after Kyle stormed out of the PPS offices to remind her that he was technically in their custody. She also wanted to bring Sara up-to-date on a new development in the case.

"Dwayne Johnson's dead."

Sara dropped her bag to the hardwood floor as she repeated Evangeline's words, then turned to gauge Kyle's reaction.

Kyle's features fell slack. "You can't honestly—"

"Is it true you left him a threatening message?"

A mix of emotion washed across Kyle's face. Shock. Uncertainty. Regret.

He nodded. "I was livid. I'd found all of the documents bearing my signature and he'd vanished from work." He ran a hand through his hair, fine lines edging the corners of his eyes. "There was no hard evidence at work. None. I figured he'd taken everything and gone underground."

He lifted his gaze to Sara's and her heart caught, stunned by the raw emotion displayed in his eyes. "He wanted to blackmail me, Sara. Blackmail me for something I didn't do."

Sara bit down on her lip and drew in a deep, slow breath. "You'd better sit down."

Kyle made a snapping noise with his mouth and started to pace in a tight pattern. "I don't need to sit down. Just tell me what you know."

"He was killed by the same caliber gun as the one that killed Jonathan Powers."

Kyle stopped, his features tensing. "My gun?"

Sara nodded. "We have to wait on ballistics, but the initial guess is yes."

"Great." He continued pacing.

"Time of death puts the murder sometime yesterday evening."

"Which coincides with the timing of my threatening message."

"There is that."

Sara stepped close, pressing her finger to Kyle's chest. Frustration and determination battled inside her. She knew the man before her was being framed, but without his help, she was never going to be able to prove anything.

"What were you thinking?" she asked softly.

Kyle looked up at the ceiling and laughed. "Who

knows what I've been thinking the past few days? I got the message from Powers, uncovered the first series of memos bearing my stolen signature and my world tilted on its side." He captured her hand in his. "And then I met you."

Sara swallowed, ignoring the tightness in her throat. As much as she wanted to jerk her fingers free of Kyle's touch, she held her ground, not wanting him to see that he affected her in the least.

For a split second, she flashed back on their kiss in the bathroom.

Kyle's move had been fueled by emotion, nothing more. She knew that. Mind over heart, she silently reminded herself.

Mind over heart.

"Did they find anything else?"

Kyle's question forced her to refocus on the here and now and not on what had transpired hours earlier.

"His home had been ransacked. Trashed."

"As if someone had been searching for something?" Kyle's voice dropped low, and if Sara wasn't mistaken dejection had begun to edge into his tone.

"Like evidence," she answered. "Evidence that someone hadn't been able to find somewhere else."

Suddenly Kyle straightened, the fire returning to his eyes. She mentally braced herself, but still wasn't prepared for the range of emotions that tangled inside her when he grasped her shoulders and gave her a quick shake.

"Can you honestly stand there and tell me you believe I murdered not one, but two men?"

His intense stare bore into hers and Sara filtered the puzzle pieces through her brain. She already knew her answer. She'd known it since the moment he'd held her in his arms at his stepfather's party. Evidence be damned.

Sara answered his question with one word. "No."

Kyle closed his eyes, wincing at her response. When he refocused on her face, Sara saw nothing but steely determination.

"What about the computer files?" She spoke her words slowly, carefully.

Kyle scowled, his eyes narrowing. "The files disappeared as I tried to access them. I've never seen anything like it. Someone knew I was in that system." He raked a hand through his hair. "I'd thought it was Johnson, but according to you, he was already dead."

"Then who?" Sara asked.

Kyle lifted his gaze to her, riveting her attention to him. "That's the question, isn't it?"

He leaned so close Sara thought he might kiss her again. The thought did odd things to her insides.

"Are you with me on this?" he asked, his voice intense.

She nodded.

"Really with me? Ready to go to TCM tomorrow and find whatever it is we can find?"

Sara nodded again. "I've been ready since the moment I got this assignment. The question—" she stepped clear of his touch before she lost control of her senses "—is whether or not you're ready?"

Kyle thinned his lips then planted his hands on his hips. "Babe, I was born ready."

"Then let's get to work." Sara headed for her overnight bag and the case file she'd shoved inside. "And stop calling me *babe*."

KYLE SAT IN AMAZEMENT at Sara's organized proficiency as she spread the documentation and evidence across the dining room table.

He hadn't yet reviewed the contents of the envelope Evangeline had handed him, but he felt no surprise when Sara explained each public record of real estate acquisitions made by Kingston Trust.

Under Kyle's signature.

The hard edge that had taken over Sara's personality was in total opposition to the feminine side she'd shown him during the days since they'd met. She relayed the facts in an almost robotlike fashion, without emotion.

He chastised himself. All that time together had been an act. And to think, he'd begun to think he might want her to stick around longer than his average conquest.

Now?

Now he sat here faced with an investigator who had infiltrated his life and was about to infiltrate his family's business empire.

But, as much as he'd tried to hold on to the anger he'd felt back at the station when she'd come clean, he couldn't stay angry with Sara.

The reality was the woman had been doing her job, and she'd done it well. Now, whether he liked it or not, she might be his only hope of avoiding conspiracy and multiple murder charges.

Kyle squeezed his eyes shut momentarily.

How had he been so blind to everything that had been going on?

"So as you can see—" Sara traced a finger down a list of land coordinates while she double-checked the figures against the notes Kyle had jotted down "—the locations are a perfect match."

"But no names." He pulled his chair closer, running the possible explanations through his mind for who could be behind this nightmare.

"None." Sara shook her head and frowned.

Kyle caught himself measuring the way her eyebrows drew together when she concentrated, the way she pressed her lips into a tight line as she studied the facts.

He tapped a finger against the list. "If the pattern continues, the next person on this list is as good as dead."

Sara nodded. "We need to check out these coordinates and find out who holds the deed."

She made a notation next to the land coordinates immediately above those she pointed to on the list.

"Powers had signed over his deed in return for cash and stock."

Kyle blew out a frustrated breath. "And look where that got him."

He looked up at Sara, startled at how close her face was to his. Her eyes widened as if the same observation had taken her by surprise.

"If I'd returned his call right away, maybe I could have—"

"Don't." Sara cut him off before he could say another word. "He thought you were behind everything. He wouldn't have let you help him."

"But if he'd listened to me—"

"Just don't."

They sat in silence for a moment.

"Why kill the investors if they've already signed over the land?" Kyle asked.

Sara glanced down at the papers, then pinned him with a knowing stare. "Part of each deal has been a share of the profits associated with Kingston Trust. So, it stands to reason that if the investors die one by one, there will be a much bigger piece of the pie for whoever survives."

"And at the end of the list?"

"One person is going to be very, very rich."

"We just have to find out who that is." Kyle sat back against his chair, putting some much-needed space between him and the subtle scent of Sara's perfume.

Sara mirrored his move, leaning away from him.

"Then your name will be cleared and the guilty party will pay."

"Sounds pretty straightforward to me." If only it could be that easy.

Sara pushed to her feet and gathered the paperwork back into the folder. "We'll soon find out. See you in the morning."

There was one topic Kyle had avoided all night. Today's kiss. The memory had hung like a specter in the air all night.

"Sara."

She stopped, turning back to look at him.

"I apologize for today." Kyle stood and walked toward her. "For kissing you. I lost my head after everything that happened."

His insides coiled into a knot. He knew full well that kissing her had not been a reaction to the day's events.

Kissing Sara had been a reaction to the desire he'd stifled since he first kissed her up on the mountain. He'd kissed her because she'd been right in front of him, voice full of hot anger, cheeks blazing with color, eyes full of passion.

If Kyle had his way, he'd kiss her again right now.

Sara gave a quick lift and drop of her shoulders. "Understood."

"Understood?"

He reached for her hand, interlacing his fingers with hers. This time when he looked into her eyes what he saw there was unmistakable.

Desire.

So blatant he could reach out and touch it.

"That it was a mistake." Sara's voice had gone soft. She pulled her hand free from Kyle's and quickly turned away. "That it won't ever happen again. Understood."

She headed down the hall toward the guest room so quickly Kyle didn't have time to tell her good night.

As he sat staring at the empty chair where she'd been moments before, he realized no matter how cool she acted, no matter how unaffected she professed to be, she felt their attraction as much as he did.

But they both knew acting on what they felt was a distraction they couldn't afford right now.

Right now, Kyle had to content himself with having Sara on his side. Hell, by his side.

When he was with Sara, Kyle felt capable of facing his demons, both known and unknown.

He felt capable of going into battle tomorrow, capable of uncovering the truth and clearing his name.

With Sara by his side, he was ready.

And as he leaned back in his chair, he laced his fingers behind his head and uttered a message for the mastermind at TCM who thought he could get away with murder.

"Bring it on."

SARA COULDN'T BELIEVE how unnerved she felt as she bolted for the emotional safety of the guest room.

Her hand felt scorched where Kyle had touched her.

She'd seen the glint in his eyes. She'd known he'd been lying about why he'd kissed her.

The more time she spent with Kyle, the more trouble she was having keeping her focus off of the man and on the case. This was crazy.

Absolutely crazy.

She dropped the folder of information and her bag onto the bed, then headed for the bathroom, grateful for the plush decor and cool tile beneath her feet.

Maybe if she tried hard enough, she could pretend she was at a five-star spa somewhere far, far away from the temptation of Kyle Prescott.

Her irrational thoughts had spiraled out of control after Kyle's kiss today, and they'd haunted her ever since. She was losing her cool.

Sara had worked countless cases during her career, cooperating with clients and coworkers alike, and no one had gotten under her skin like Kyle had in just a few short days.

What was it about the man?

His arrogance? His confidence?

The way his eyes seemed to see right through the tough shell she'd worked so hard to perfect?

The way that—even through his playboy facade— she knew deep down he was a regular guy?

She leaned toward the oversized mirror as she brushed her teeth, blowing out an exasperated sigh.

If Evangeline could see her now, she'd no doubt

give Sara another disapproving shake of her head. The woman was a genius when it came to reading people, and she'd spotted Sara's weakness for Kyle from the beginning of the investigation.

Perhaps Sara should have removed herself from the case once she felt the first glimmer of attraction.

But, she hadn't. Nor did she want to.

What she wanted was to break this case wide open.

She rinsed out her toothbrush then splashed cold water on her face. Today, she'd skipped the full repertoire of makeup her undercover persona had required she wear during the past few days, relieved to do so.

Sara stripped out of her clothing and shrugged into her favorite nightshirt. She anchored her hair up into a ponytail and pulled out the folder of notes one more time.

Tomorrow was the day that could very well make this case, and she wanted to be prepared for anything, and anyone.

Her cell phone beeped and she reached for her bag, smiling when she saw the text message waiting.

The PPS crew had sent her additional information on the infrastructure of TCM, for which Sara was more than thankful.

But as she settled down to work, she realized she wasn't thankful for the new information as it related to the case.

No.

She was thankful for the distraction the new material offered from her thoughts of Kyle Prescott.

Her unrelenting, conflicted thoughts.

Had her feelings for Kyle tainted how she'd handled the case so far?

Perhaps.

Another investigator might not have been so quick to believe a suspect's innocence when all of the evidence pointed to his guilt. Yet, Sara knew she was correct.

She knew Kyle was being framed.

Tomorrow would be a new day, and tomorrow she'd keep her focus exactly where it belonged.

On the case and nowhere else.

Certainly not on Kyle Prescott in any other capacity than a falsely accused man in need of vindication.

Chapter Eleven

Kyle wasn't prepared for the sight that greeted him when he stepped into his kitchen the next morning. Sara had made a simple breakfast of eggs and bacon and the smell of fresh-brewed coffee filled the air. The woman herself was a sight for sore eyes.

She'd pulled her wavy hair back into a clip, exposing the long, smooth expanse of her neck. Kyle's traitorous gut tightened and he flashed back on his sleepless night, in which he'd entertained countless fantasies about retracting his statement that kissing her had been a mistake.

Sara had dressed conservatively, yet she'd certainly let her femininity shine. A fitted white shirt disappeared into the nipped waist of a knee-length black skirt. A matching jacket sat draped over the back of a kitchen chair. Her feet, however, were bare.

If someone had told Kyle a week ago that he'd be waking to a barefoot personal security expert making breakfast in his kitchen, he'd have called them insane. But now?

"Forget your shoes?" he asked as he dropped his own jacket over the chair next to Sara's.

She poured a steaming mug of coffee and tipped her head toward the hallway as she handed the mug to Kyle.

Kyle followed her gesture then let out a long, low whistle.

A pair of knee-high turquoise boots sat propped against the wall.

"Part of your uniform?"

"When in Rome." Her lips quirked into a crooked smile.

Kyle took a sip of the coffee, nodded his appreciation then furrowed his brow. "You're telling me that you think those—" he jerked his thumb toward the hall "—boots are standard accessories for TCM?" He let out a chuckle. "I don't think so."

"Let me ask you this, Mr. Prescott."

Sara leaned across the kitchen island and it took every ounce of willpower Kyle possessed not to look at the way her shirt must be straining across her breasts.

Based on the sparkle in her eyes, she knew exactly what she was doing.

"As a TCM executive who's never met me before, would you be more receptive to my questions if I were wearing a pair of no-nonsense pumps, or those?" She tipped her head toward the hall.

Kyle made a snapping noise with his mouth. "Can't argue with that logic."

"Very well, then." Sara straightened and turned away. "Hurry up and eat. We've got a big day ahead of us."

KYLE AND SARA had spent the morning questioning TCM employees under the guise of corporate identity assessment. Their efforts had gotten them nowhere.

He'd left her in his office now, working through the in-house computer system, while he set out to work his in-house contacts.

Visits to Investor Relations, Information Systems and Business Planning had gotten him nowhere. Sure, he hadn't been able to come straight out and ask about the name Kingston Trust or the recent land deals, but no one had mentioned either when discussing recent TCM transactions.

The omission told Kyle that none of the department heads knew a thing about what had gone on, and that fact implied what Kyle had suspected all along.

There was a rogue on the inside.

Someone smart enough and fearless enough to impersonate Kyle and orchestrate multimillion-dollar deals under the phony identity of Kingston Trust.

But who?

Kyle steadied his breath as he stood outside his stepfather's office.

He and the man had never been close. He made

no attempts to deny that. But in the past, even normal conversations typically turned strained.

He needed to keep his cool today. Needed to question Stephen about the direction TCM had taken during the past few months. He needed to find a way to extract information about TCM investments and business deals without appearing obvious.

Kyle stood poised to enter the CEO's suite of offices to face his stepfather. He drew in a steadying breath, straightened and pushed through the door.

"Kyle." His stepfather's executive assistant, Mary Jane Simpson, greeted him with a warm smile.

If he didn't know better, he'd swear the look was intended exclusively for him. Based on experience, Kyle knew the expression was one Mary Jane had perfected over years of working in the office. Everyone who walked through that door received the same beaming welcome.

"Mary Jane." Kyle returned the greeting and tipped his chin toward the door to Stephen Turner's private office. "I need to speak with him."

Mary Jane pursed her lips. "Sorry, dear. He's out with investors looking at some property. I don't expect him back today."

A disbelieving laugh burst through Kyle's lips. What were the odds? He hadn't set foot inside TCM in months and when he finally did, his stepfather was out. *With investors.*

"What kind of property?" he asked, curiosity edging out his disappointment at missing the chance to question Stephen.

"Land, I believe." Mary Jane blew out a sigh, and gave a quick shake of her tightly permed, overly bleached curls. "You know your stepfather. Always wheeling and dealing, working to grow the empire, as I call it."

Her laughter rang sour in Kyle's ears.

Could Stephen be behind the conspiracy? Was he capable of negotiating for land rights, then killing the previous owners?

Kyle couldn't picture it, but money did strange things to people.

According to Sara's information, the land that had been acquired was worth a fortune, to put it mildly, just for the value of the oil that lay beneath the rocky surface.

"Would you leave him a message that I was here?"

"Of course, dear."

Kyle was still trying to picture his stepfather as a criminal mastermind when he stepped back out into the hall and directly into the broad chest of Buddy Forman.

"Fancy meeting you here," Forman snarled, his raspy voice instantly grating on Kyle's nerves.

"I work here." Kyle stepped away from the man's bulk. "I'd suggest you remember that."

"I get the feeling you're looking for something." Buddy moved to block Kyle's path. "Might I suggest you stop?"

Kyle laughed, a bitter burst of air he hoped clearly conveyed his disgust with the man.

"You can suggest all you want, but I have no plans to listen."

"What about Johnson?" Buddy straightened, as if he knew some secret. "From what I understand, he's already found what you're looking for."

That was the problem, wasn't it? Kyle knew Johnson had found those files, but what had he done with the hard copies after he destroyed the computer files?

Kyle stepped around Buddy, headed back toward his office and Sara, but he stopped, suddenly tempted to trick Buddy into spilling what he knew about Dwayne Johnson's murder. His gut told him Forman knew plenty.

But he couldn't.

Johnson had no family and the police department had purposely put a lid on announcing the murder, hoping to draw out the killer through the lack of media attention.

"Something you wanted to say?" Forman asked.

"No, actually. Have a nice day," Kyle called out over his shoulder as he strode away.

He'd struck out on every level today, from subtle questions to out-and-out file searches.

He and Sara obviously weren't going to find their answers playing by the rules. They were going to have to take a different approach.

Kyle smiled to himself as he neared his office.

He knew exactly what they needed to do.

And when.

SARA FELT the pair of eyes burning through her scalp before she looked up.

Peter Turner stood at the door, a veritable leer plastered on his face.

The small hairs at the back of Sara's neck pricked to attention, and she blew out a steadying breath. The man might give her the creeps, but he'd seen Annemarie during her last day alive. She might as well use his unwanted interest to her advantage.

"This is a pleasant surprise." She stood, rounding the desk, hand extended.

Peter took her hand in his, gave it a quick pump then held it, as he had at Stephen Turner's party, until Sara eased her fingers free of his grip.

"I hear you're our new image consultant." Amusement danced in Peter's emerald eyes.

Sara would almost have called his eyes stunning, were it not for a lurking coolness in the depths of his gaze. His dark blond hair fell into impeccably trimmed layers, just as it had the first night they'd met.

The man was a poster boy for the polished appearance money could buy.

Sara nodded. "Yes. I'm looking at a full identity

overhaul for TCM, and not a moment too soon, I might add."

She pointed to the display of brochures and investor documents she'd spread across the desk as camouflage. Truth be told, the materials were nothing but classy, and perfectly conveyed the image of a successful corporation on the rise.

They didn't require an iota of change.

But Peter Turner didn't need to know that.

"What do you suggest we do to remedy the situation?" Peter asked, moving close. Too close.

Sara increased the space between them by moving back behind the desk, putting the expansive teak piece between them. The disappointment in Peter's expression was instant.

The display on the computer monitor caught Sara's peripheral vision.

Damn.

She'd been fishing in the system when Peter had made his appearance. If he caught a glimpse of the screen and figured out what she was really doing at TCM, he'd no doubt blow her cover sky-high.

Sara tapped on a copy of TCM's annual report to shift Peter's focus to the slick cover.

"Do you see this?" She pointed to the logo, waiting until she was certain Peter's gaze had landed on the same spot. "It's all wrong for today's business environment."

With her other hand, she reached for the keyboard, pressing the command key to put the screen into hibernation.

"Today's mega-company wants to convey brightness, success, youth," she continued, hoping her bull-slinging wasn't as obvious as it felt.

Her heart had begun to pound and she worked to control her breathing. She couldn't afford to have this man think he affected her or intimidated her.

The monitor's display went black and Sara breathed a mental sigh of relief.

"The materials are dated." She shrugged. "It's quite a disappointment, actually."

Sara looked up from the desk, putting on her most serious I-know-exactly-what-I'm-talking-about expression as she waited for Peter to shift his gaze back to her face.

"It's an interesting concept," he said as he lifted his head. "I'm sure someone as lovely as yourself knows everything there is to know about image. My father will be pleased. Wherever did Kyle find you?"

"At your father's party," she answered coyly.

Peter leaned across the desk and Sara crossed her arms, her nonverbal message loud and clear.

"Pity my brother saw you first." He let out a low, long whistle. "You Montgomery girls must be the prettiest things in this part of Colorado."

Sara fought the urge to reach across the desk and grab the arrogant man by his throat.

Instead she backed up to lean her hip against

Kyle's credenza. "Aren't you sweet." She forced the words through gritted teeth, smiling all the while.

Then she seized the opportunity to narrow their conversation's focus to Annemarie.

"I was surprised to hear you knew my sister. You're so much younger than she would have been."

Peter shrugged, his eyebrows crooking toward his too-perfect hairline. "I was just a kid, but she was always nice to me."

Always.

"So you'd met her before?"

He pursed his lips as if searching his memory. "My parents dragged me to most every party in town back then, so yes, I'm sure I met her on more than one occasion."

"And that last time—" Sara hesitated, wanting to choose her words very carefully "—did you happen to notice anything odd, or anyone spending an unusual amount of time with my sister?"

"Haunted by the past, Sara?"

She rankled, offended by the palpable note of enjoyment in the man's voice.

"I suppose I am," she answered truthfully. "I just wondered whether you'd spoken to the police after her death. Whether they'd question such a small child."

"Your sister was very much alive when I left that party, Ms. Montgomery. The police had no cause to question me."

Peter tensed, and the amusement in his eyes faded, replaced by a shuttered glare.

Sara noted the change in his tone and the way he addressed her instantly. Something she'd said had hit a nerve and put him on edge.

Peter turned to leave. "After all—" he hesitated at the door "—who's going to believe anything a five-year-old has to say?"

He was gone before Sara could tell him that she would have, and she would now. She'd take anything he could remember, and she was certain he remembered something.

His mood had shifted sharply and quickly, and it hadn't been because of her criticism of the annual report.

No.

Peter Turner had stiffened as soon as she'd mentioned the police.

He was hiding something.

Sara had only to figure out what.

WHEN KYLE REALIZED his brother was making a move to leave the office, he slipped into the next doorway and out of sight.

He was in no mood for Peter or for anything his half brother might have to say.

As bothered as he was by his encounter with Buddy Forman, he was more concerned about the emotion in Sara's voice as she'd spoken to Peter.

If the imbecile had done anything to upset or offend her, he'd wring Peter's neck with his bare hands.

Kyle caught himself before he stepped out into the open and into his office. Heat flared in his face and he realized he'd come to care about Sara and her feelings more than he'd like to admit.

The truth was, as much as the woman tried to project an impenetrable shell, her vulnerability hid just below the surface.

Peter's question about being haunted by her sister's death had apparently opened a crevice in her calm, cool demeanor.

Kyle made the conscious decision to say nothing about what he'd overheard. He'd known Sara long enough to realize she liked her private life to be just that. Private. He'd keep their conversation focused where it belonged.

On Kingston Trust. And on the missing files.

"Ready to go?" he asked as he breezed into his office.

Sara sat at his desk, working at the keyboard, her forehead creased with deep concentration.

"Sure," she answered. "But I haven't found a thing yet. You?"

"Zip," Kyle answered. "But I have a plan."

Sara's attention snapped from the monitor to Kyle, her lovely features shifting into an expression of pure curiosity. "You have a plan?"

"I do." Kyle grinned. "And you, Ms. Montgomery, are going to love it."

AN UNMISTAKABLE TENSION emanated from Sara on the ride home. Kyle had tried to engage her in conversation unrelated to the case as a distraction, but he'd failed.

She sat staring out the passenger window, lost in her own world. No doubt lost in her haunting memories.

Kyle longed to reach out and take her hand. Longed to entwine his fingers in hers and squeeze, offering a reassuring word that everything would be all right.

But he couldn't make her that promise.

He hadn't yet accepted his father's death and still carried the guilt of never telling the man how much he cared.

How could he help Sara accept her sister's death? How could he help expunge her demons when he'd never managed to lose his own?

At long last, Sara turned to face him, a forced smile turning up the corners of her mouth. "You mentioned a plan?"

Kyle smiled, reaching reflexively for her before realizing what he'd done. He caught himself just as his palm brushed her knee.

"A brilliant plan," he answered.

He regripped the wheel of his sports car as if nothing had happened.

"You and I are going to break into TCM and access the system's mainframe."

Sara squinted, smiling slightly. "Why would the head of the international division have to break in?"

"We don't know who we're up against, correct?" he asked.

Sara nodded.

"Then we can't operate during normal business hours. We'll go back tonight and access the hard drives."

"And you know how to do all of this?"

Kyle shot her a grin. "That's where you come in. You and your PPS connections."

Sara sat quietly for a few minutes, eyes narrowed, concentrating.

"You might be on to something." When she finally spoke, her tone had dropped low and intent. "I'll stop by PPS and see what we need to do. If anyone will know how to access deleted files on that system, they will."

"Excellent."

"You'll take care of getting us inside?" This time, Sara's voice climbed a few octaves.

Kyle laughed.

"I'll take care of getting us inside."

He'd just started a blow-by-blow description of how they'd bypass security when he realized they weren't alone on the road.

That fact wasn't unusual, especially for this time of

day, but it was the type of vehicle and the speed with which it was gaining on them that raised his suspicions.

The vehicle looming in his rearview was none other than a large black SUV, eerily reminiscent of the truck that had run them off the mountain the first time they'd met.

Buddy Forman? If Kyle didn't know better, he'd think so, but he wasn't about to wait around to find out.

"Hold on."

Sara did as she was told, reaching up to brace herself against the passenger door.

Kyle waited until their car was aligned with a turnoff up into the mountains, then he cut the wheel, sending dirt and rocks flying. As he downshifted and gunned the engine, he risked a glance in the rearview mirror.

The cumbersome SUV had attempted to follow, but had run up on the shoulder and now sat, apparently stalled, in a cloud of dust.

Kyle pressed the accelerator to the floor, taking the next turnoff, and the next.

He left nothing to chance. He knew these back mountain roads like he knew the lines of his own palm, and he knew how to lose a tail.

Twenty minutes later, they arrived at his property. Kyle slowed the car as they approached, wanting to make sure they didn't have company waiting in the form of a black SUV.

The drive sat empty.

Kyle quickly maneuvered the car behind the house and into the garage.

Apparently the coast was clear for now, and he could only hope it stayed that way.

Obviously whoever had given chase knew the car belonged to Kyle. If their pursuer wanted to push the envelope, he no doubt knew where Kyle lived and knew where to find him.

The thought didn't scare Kyle.

Oddly, it excited him, made him feel more alive than he'd felt in years.

He was ready for a fight. Ready for a battle. He'd do whatever it took to reclaim his honor and his name, and no one, not even some thug in a large SUV, was going to take that away from him.

There was only one thing that might slow him down.

He studied the proud set of Sara's shoulders as she walked in front of him as they closed the distance between the garage and the home's back entrance.

That one thing was Sara.

She might be a professional, but now that she'd become entangled in the nightmare conspiracy at TCM, she could very well become a target.

If at any time he realized her life was in danger, his game plan would shift. Sara's safety took priority over everything else.

Honor and name be damned.

He'd sacrifice both if it meant saving Sara's life.

The very thought sobered him more than any forged signature or murder charge ever could.

Chapter Twelve

Both Kyle and Sara had changed into dark jeans and black turtlenecks for their return appearance at the offices of TCM.

Sara had paid a visit to PPS and they were fully coached and equipped for their mission.

Retrieving the deleted files from the TCM computer network.

They approached the back entrance silently, moving along the wall of the building to avoid being in direct view of the security camera.

"Are you sure you've got the current access code?" Sara asked.

"Completely," Kyle whispered, gesturing for Sara to be quiet.

"It's just that it's probably been a while—"

"I have the code." This time his whisper grew louder, harsher.

"What about the system? Will it log you as entering?"

It wasn't that she didn't trust the man, but she needed to be sure he'd thought every detail through.

"Only if you keep talking loud enough to trigger the sound alarms."

Sara fell silent, but glared at Kyle's profile as he entered the code into the alarm panel. The doors clicked and he grinned.

He pulled the security door open, motioning for Sara to enter.

"Ladies first," he whispered as she brushed past him.

An unwanted shiver danced across her shoulders and she reminded herself for the umpteenth time that her job was to uncover the truth and clear Kyle. Nothing more.

After this investigation was closed, she'd more than likely never see the man again.

Heaven knew they didn't travel in the same social circles.

Kyle eased the door shut behind them, clicked on his flashlight, then rearmed the system.

"Motion detectors?" Sara whispered as she illuminated her own lantern.

Kyle shook his head. "System's not geared for that." He tipped his chin down the hall and Sara followed, nervous energy vibrating inside her.

As she followed Kyle, she ran through the list of instructions she'd been given by the tech experts at PPS. According to Kyle, there had existed a mountain of evidence where there now was nothing.

All Sara had to do was figure out a way to make the system sing.

She thought again briefly of the agent PPS had lost. The man who never met a computer system he couldn't beat. Lenny. How she wished he were with her now.

She cast a glance heavenward and shot up a silent prayer.

Who knew? Maybe he'd be with her after all.

She and Kyle worked their way through the TCM offices at a steady pace, not wanting to make any unnecessary noise, although Kyle had made it quite clear no one would see or hear them in this section of the building.

The security monitors covered the front entrance and the executive suites only. Even if the guard was still awake, a rare occurrence apparently, he'd have no idea he had company in the far recesses of the property.

They'd decided on flashlights as a precaution on the off chance someone driving by might see lights on and alert the police or security.

Sara found the resulting effect both eerie and enthralling.

The beams of their flashlights bounced from doorway to doorway, casting shadows as they passed file cabinets and office plants, cubicles and expensive artwork.

She hadn't done much breaking and entering— not that this really counted considering she was with one of the company's vice presidents—but the darkened space and sense of impending discovery sent a thrill racing through her.

They were close to what they needed.

She could feel it.

Her stomach had begun an anxious tumble when Kyle turned to her and gave her the signal.

Thumbs up.

He'd located the mainframe.

Now it was Sara's turn to perform.

She worked from memory, doing her best to cover each step the PPS computer specialist had taught her.

She first entered the TCM system using Kyle's access code, then bypassed the system, choosing to operate in the rudimentary computer language that had once been the only game in town.

She squeezed her eyes shut momentarily and pictured the series of commands she needed to input. When she snapped her eyes open once more, Kyle's face was so close to hers she had to stifle a gasp.

He held up his hands, apparently realizing he'd moved too close. He mouthed the word "sorry" as he stepped behind her to lean over her shoulder instead.

Sara had been impressed by his determination and dedication to uncovering the truth behind the TCM conspiracy.

Another man—especially one so young—might have done anything necessary to cover up the problem, to save the company from any unwanted financial or legal complications, yet Kyle had insisted on one thing from the beginning.

The truth.

Impressive for a twenty-eight-year-old.

Sara shoved the wayward thought out of her head and input the first series of commands.

A small box appeared on the screen. Sara reached into her pocket and pulled out the tiny device she'd picked up at PPS.

She pressed a button to extend the USB connection, then found an available slot on the front of the system.

She slipped the device into the opening, checked the fit, then input the second set of commands.

She pushed Enter.

Nothing happened.

"Damn," she muttered under her breath.

"Try again," Kyle whispered in her ear, his breath sending the small hairs on her neck lifting to attention. "Take your time."

Sara did as he suggested, retyping the command. She saw her mistake as soon as she keyed it in. An extra space. She made the adjustment and hit Enter.

This time the box vanished and a list of root files appeared.

"We'll back everything up as soon as we find them," she whispered.

"But I want hard copies, as well," Kyle said. "Call me old-fashioned, but this time I want evidence I can put my hands on."

"Agreed."

Sara scanned the list, selecting the directory where deleted files often remained unless someone smart enough went into the system and wiped them clean.

She entered the command to open the directory, breathing a sigh of relief when a rather endless list appeared.

"Can you sort by date?" This time Kyle's breath brushed against her neck and Sara wished he'd move far enough away that she wasn't aware of his every move.

"Not a problem," she whispered.

A few seconds later, the deed was done.

She scrolled back two days and instantly recognized the welcome memo files she'd spotted on Kyle's computer the first time she'd sneaked a look.

"Do you see them all?" she asked.

Kyle pressed a palm to her shoulder, sending a jolt through her system. Sara scolded herself and did her best to focus solely on the screen before them.

Kyle traced the list of file names with his free hand, muttering under his breath as he did so. "Yes. You've done it. We've got them now."

The overhead lights flashed on just as he lifted his finger from the screen.

"Jackpot," Sara murmured at the same moment. "What the—"

She spun toward the door just as Kyle launched himself into position, shielding her body with his own, as if they were about to go down in a barrage of gunfire.

Stephen Turner was the last person she expected to see. But there he stood, arms crossed, a look of disbelief on his face.

The overhead light made his dark brown hair gleam, but his dark eyes shone with something completely different.

Fury.

"What in the hell is going on?"

KYLE STRAIGHTENED and mirrored his stepfather's body language. "I might ask you the same thing."

Stephen Turner frowned, anger flashing in his eyes. "I'm going to go out on a limb and surmise that this stunt has something to do with your visit to the offices today."

"Correct." Kyle nodded.

Stephen frowned. "Start talking."

Kyle jerked his thumb toward the computer screen. "Are you aware of this?"

"Of you breaking into the system? Yes." Stephen covered the width of the room in only a few strides. "What are *you* talking about?"

"This." Sara tapped the screen.

Kyle started talking and didn't stop until he'd covered everything from the Kingston Trust welcome memos to the land-acquisition documents, all bearing his stolen electronic signature.

He knew he was taking a risk if Stephen was the mastermind behind the conspiracy, but his gut instinct told him no.

Based on Stephen's reaction, Kyle's gut had been correct.

"My company will be ruined." Stephen sank into an available chair. "How would someone do this?"

"That's what we're trying to figure out," Sara answered. "We have a list of land coordinates, but no names." She pointed to the screen. "Unfortunately, these documents don't provide any names, either, but they do corroborate what we've uncovered so far. They also clearly show that someone's buying up oil-rich property left and right."

"Under my company's name." Stephen's voice had gone flat.

"Under the guise of Kingston Investments," Sara explained. "A blind trust operated by someone within your company."

"Someone with the capability of accessing the key to your signature?"

Kyle met his stepfather's questioning gaze and nodded.

"I thought Dwayne Johnson might be behind this—" Kyle's words trailed away.

"He was found murdered yesterday." Sara delivered the news. "The police haven't made the crime public yet, so I'd appreciate your discretion."

All color drained from Stephen's face. "My God."

"There's one more thing." Sara's voice turned soft, more gentle than Kyle had yet heard it. "At least four investors were eliminated once their deals were complete."

"Eliminated?" Stephen's features tensed and his throat worked.

"Murdered," Sara answered.

"Are you involved?" His stepfather leveled a look at Kyle, his expression a cross between disappointment and shock.

Kyle shook his head. "Someone's trying to set me up. These hard copies all point the finger of guilt at me, but I'm innocent." He dropped his voice. "I want to clear my name. I want to clear the company's name."

"We might be able to find our mastermind by tracing the money," Sara added. "If we're lucky, everything we need will be buried in these pages."

"I'm sorry you felt stealth was the only way to get the information you needed."

If Kyle weren't mistaken, the emotion splayed across his stepfather's face was nothing short of true regret.

"I'm sorry you didn't feel you could ask me for help," his stepfather continued.

Kyle swallowed, suddenly aware of all the years that had slipped away, years during which the two men had remained strangers instead of family.

"I'm sorry." Kyle's voice sounded defeated, tired, even to his own ears. "Maybe you can help us now."

As he uttered the statement, Sara's surprised look didn't escape his notice. She turned away, entering a command that sent the main printer humming to life.

"You have my full support," Stephen said. "Whatever you need...son."

The word sounded odd to Kyle's ears, but he accepted it. Maybe in time...

He trained his gaze on Sara and her fingers flying across the keyboard. "We need to keep this between us. We have no idea of who we're dealing with."

"Understood," his stepfather answered. "I suppose it could be anyone inside TCM."

"Whoever is behind this will know we've printed off the documents." Kyle shook his head as he watched sheets of paper pile into the printer's output tray.

A sly look spread across his stepfather's face. "Not if we override the tracking program."

Kyle matched Stephen's expression with a slight grin. "Genius."

But as he moved toward the printer to gather the documents, it was another of his stepfather's phrases that echoed in his mind.

I suppose it could be anyone.

He was absolutely right.

That was the problem.

Chapter Thirteen

Hours later Kyle and Sara sat at his dining room table once again, this time scrutinizing the pile of printed documents sorted by land coordinates.

Target assessments.

Hidden property analyses.

Purchase directives.

Agreements of sale.

The paper trail they'd gathered was thorough. It was organized. And it was complete. There was only one thing missing.

"No names." Sara blew out the statement on a sigh.

Kyle gave a quick shake of his head. "Not one."

"Obviously we can match the land coordinates to the deed holder—" she pointed to the piles of paperwork associated with each of the murder victims "—and we know the names for these coordinates."

She pulled the master list front and center on the table. "We need to start here. Identify and warn the next person on this list before our body count increases."

"What if we're too late?" Kyle asked.

Sara sucked in her lower lip. "No agreement of sale." She tapped the pile. "Whoever owns this land is safe until they sign on the dotted line."

She sat back as if another thought had just hit her. "Maybe we should force whoever is behind all of this out into the open. Let them know we're on to them."

"How?"

"By warning whoever we can, by asking questions. Let's let word trickle back to them that we're not going away."

"What about the money trail?" Kyle leaned forward, looking for the sales agreements and any indication of where the final payments had gone.

"They were very careful. Everything goes through the trust," Sara answered. "But one of the investor's agreements showed an account number."

She fished through the sheets of paper, smiling when she found what she wanted. She slid the paper toward Kyle.

"Offshore account." His pulse picked up a notch. Could they finally be closing in? *"Cuerva."*

"Cuerva." Sara's smile widened. "I'll call Evangeline first thing tomorrow and get the ball rolling on this."

"And when we find out who holds that account?"

"We find out who's been buying up all of Colorado's oil-rich land and knocking off the competition."

Their gazes met and locked, their shared excitement undeniable.

Kyle fought the urge to pull Sara into a hug. Instead he turned back to the evidence. "Until we find our man…"

"We do our best to avoid any new victims," Sara said, finishing his thought. "It's amazing what greed will do to some people, isn't it?"

Kyle nodded. "You'd think those in control would be focused on preserving the land, not stockpiling it like some disposable possession."

Sara's expression shifted, the excitement in her eyes giving way to a hint of anger. "You should put your money where your mouth is."

"How do you know I don't?"

Kyle bristled defensively. This was the last thing he needed right now. A lecture on using his riches charitably.

"Do you?" One brown eyebrow lifted in question.

He thought about stretching the truth, but there wasn't any truth to stretch. "No." Kyle bolstered himself, speaking confidently and strongly, realizing her lecture was right on the mark. "Maybe it's time I start taking part in my community."

"Instead of taking part in the party scene?"

He leveled a gaze at her, surprised by her remark. "Where did that come from?"

Sara shook her head. "Sorry. I'm just exhausted." She waved a hand dismissively. "Sorry."

But Kyle chose not to let the topic go. "Why do you have such a big chip on your shoulder?"

"Against you?"

Kyle shook his head. "Against the society scene in general."

A range of emotion washed across Sara's face. Anger. Uncertainty. Grief.

She put her face close to Kyle's, meeting his stare head-on. "If the beautiful people didn't hold themselves in such high esteem then maybe the rest of us wouldn't have to lose ourselves trying to fit in."

Kyle laughed. Sara frowned in response.

"You've never tried to fit in a day in your life," he said.

Sara's only answer was the hint of moisture gathering in her pale eyes.

Kyle's heart caught, but he fought the urge to gather her into his arms. He knew better. If she thought he'd seen any sign of weakness in her, they'd never find a way to bridge the gap between them.

"Your sister?" he asked softly.

Sara nodded. "Her death will haunt me until the day I die."

Kyle took her hand in his. "Tell me what happened. Please."

She shook her head. "I promised myself a long time ago that I'd let go."

"But you obviously haven't." Kyle squeezed her hand, then pulled their joined hands to his chest. His heart pounded through his shirt, but he made no move to hide it. "I overheard your conversation with Peter."

"You were eavesdropping?" Color fired in Sara's cheeks.

"No." Kyle pulled her closer still. Warmth uncoiled inside him when Sara didn't pull away. "I just happened to overhear. It was an accident."

"Sorry." Sara dropped her chin and shook her head. "That was unfair."

Kyle hooked his fingers beneath her chin and tugged her focus to his face. "Let me help you." He dropped his hand from her chin, capturing her other hand in his.

Sara searched his face, as if she weren't quite sure she'd heard him correctly. When she finally spoke, her words surprised Kyle.

"Your brother, Peter, knows something, but he isn't talking."

Kyle squinted. "He couldn't have been more than five."

"But he saw something." Now it was Sara who tightened her grip on his hands. "I questioned him and he clammed up when I asked about the police. When I asked what he'd seen." She shook his hands. "He knows something, Kyle."

"Then I'll do whatever I can to get it out of him." He grimaced a bit. "You do realize there's no love lost between us, so I can't promise I'll have any success."

She nodded then smiled hopefully. "Just the fact you're willing to try is enough for me."

SILENCE FELL between them again and Sara realized they'd just taken their relationship to a new level.

This one personal.

She decided to push the envelope a bit more.

"Why do you think there's such tension between you and your parents?"

The question made Kyle visibly flinch.

"Which ones?" He blew out a sharp breath. "Maybe that question sums up the whole problem."

"You never saw your father once Olivia brought you back to the States?"

"Not until a few years ago," Kyle answered as though the response were a reflex, as though he'd thought about that particular question countless times.

"We were just rebuilding our relationship when he was killed." He laughed bitterly. "I never told him how much he meant to me, and now he's gone."

Sara studied the floor for a moment, shoving aside her own grief for Robert Prescott to make way for Kyle's. She couldn't imagine what it would feel like to lose a parent. She could only guess based on the grief that lingered in her heart for Annemarie.

"I'm sorry."

"No one ever said life was fair." Kyle forced a smile, but Sara wasn't buying the sincerity of the expression for a moment.

Now that Kyle was talking, the investigator in her couldn't stop pressing for information.

"What about you and Stephen Turner?"

Kyle made a snapping noise with his mouth. "Never close. He had Peter to worry about…and my mother. He had his hands full.

"I used to think he thought I could take care of myself, but then one day I began to wonder if he made so little time for me simply because he didn't care."

Sara tucked a hair that had slipped out of her ponytail behind her ear. "He doesn't strike me as an unfeeling sort of man."

She thought back to the birthday party and the gentle way he'd handled Olivia's outburst.

"I wouldn't call it unfeeling." Kyle squinted as if searching for the perfect word. "I'd call it apathetic."

"So you decided to take your title at TCM and play hooky?"

He nodded very slowly, eyebrows raised. "I guess that's exactly how it looks, isn't it?"

"I'd say that's exactly what you did."

"Touché."

Kyle laughed a deep, rumbling laugh that sent the heat simmering inside Sara into a full boil.

"So I guess this means we're both loners." Sara pulled one hand free from Kyle's to trace her fingertip down his cheek.

"Maybe not."

As he spoke the words he leaned forward, lightly brushing Sara's lips with his own.

The desire that had built inside her for days began

to unwind, edging through her system with a white-hot need like none she'd ever known.

All her thoughts on remaining objective and on avoiding any involvement with Kyle were lost as his tongue found hers, tangling and tasting.

He grasped her upper arms, pulling her to him. Sara wound her fingers behind his neck and into the unkempt hair she'd grown to love.

Kyle trailed his kisses down the length of her neck to the soft hollow at the base of her throat. From somewhere deep inside she moaned with pleasure, but she didn't care.

She didn't care that he'd finally seen the side of her she'd so carefully protected for so long.

Sara wanted to be with him, fully with him. Of that, she was one hundred percent sure.

Kyle broke their kiss and stood, taking Sara's hand and leading her toward his bedroom. Her determination to be with him faltered for a moment when she imagined how many other women—younger women—he'd led down this same hall.

As if he'd read her mind, Kyle turned to face her, pressing a soft kiss to her forehead.

"Rumors of my past escapades have been greatly exaggerated."

She laughed softly then tipped her chin to meet his mouth, this time taking charge, pressing his lips apart and tasting deeply.

Kyle backed her against the wall and everything shifted.

Theirs was a collision of hands and mouths, tongues tangling, bodies pressing one against the other, an explosion of pent-up attraction and tension and the desire for the ultimate release.

Kyle scooped her into his arms, carrying her effortlessly to his bedroom and onto his bed. Sara pulled off her shirt and unfastened her jeans, as Kyle did the same.

They matched each other's moves, both undressing as fast as they could, their eyes locked, their focus never leaving one another.

Sara's breath came fast and shallow as Kyle lowered himself on top of her, gently pressing the hard lines of his body into her soft curves.

She bit down on her lip at the feel of his erection against her stomach. She reveled in the quickening of Kyle's breath, in the knowledge she'd brought him to such a state of desire just by being who she was and not by being the undercover debutante she'd pretended to be just days before.

"Typically, I'm much more chivalrous than what I'm about to be." He grinned, pressing a kiss to Sara's lips. "But I've been waiting for this since the moment I first saw you."

Hot desire pooled heavy inside Sara and she thought she might explode just from the sound of Kyle's voice.

She met his grin with her own. "So what are you waiting for?"

He lowered himself between her legs, and Sara opened her body to him, welcoming his gentle thrust as he pushed inside her.

Sara's breath caught at the sensation of their bodies joining, of Kyle's breath against her neck, his hands planted to either side of her head, his heart beating against her own.

He moved slowly at first, tenderly, as if he might have full control over his body's reaction, but then his movements intensified, quickened.

Sara matched him thrust for thrust, losing herself to the mind-numbing edge of release on which she balanced. When Kyle slid his hands beneath her and angled her body into his, she lost all control, her orgasm exploding through her, ripping away her every last thread of defense.

Kyle followed immediately, shuddering with his release. He never let go, never loosened his hold on her, keeping her close, whispering tender words as they drifted off to sleep.

Together.

SARA WOKE in the middle of the night, startled by the feel of Kyle's arms wrapped around her. She stiffened momentarily then relaxed, letting herself settle into his embrace, her back to his stomach.

Sheltered.

Safe.

Her body hummed from their lovemaking. Satiated. Relaxed and at ease.

She'd suspected since the moment he first shook her hand that they'd end up here. Together. Intimate.

She just hadn't imagined it would be so soon, or in the middle of their investigation.

Regret tangled with the pleasure inside her.

Sara imagined that she and Kyle wouldn't have enough in common to keep any sort of a relationship going once the investigation was over.

Perhaps for once in her life she'd be able to enjoy the here and now, to take whatever pleasure she could while it lasted.

It was better that way.

She'd done just fine by herself so far. Why complicate her life with a long-term involvement?

Her insides belied her thoughts, twisting at the mere thought of not seeing Kyle again once the case was solved.

She shifted in his arms, turning to see his sleeping face, to study the lines of his jaw and the curl of his hair against his cheek.

She'd put his life in danger by letting him get so involved in the investigation.

Once she'd revealed her true identity, she should have kept him at arm's length, using him for information and connections only.

What if it hadn't been Stephen Turner who found them hacking into the mainframe?

What if it had been the true mastermind behind the conspiracy? The person who obviously wouldn't hesitate to commit murder to protect his or her identity?

There was no telling what might have happened.

Sara traced her fingertip lightly down Kyle's cheek and then along his jaw.

She cared for this man even more deeply than she'd suspected. If she didn't know better, she'd think Kyle Prescott had begun to steal her heart. Something no man had ever done before.

The realization made Sara's next steps crystal clear.

She'd leave tomorrow before he woke up.

She'd check out the land coordinates on her own.

She'd do her job.

Without him.

It was the only way she knew to keep Kyle safe.

And suddenly keeping him safe had taken precedence over everything else.

Chapter Fourteen

Sara woke the next morning a bit before six. She slipped out of bed then pulled Kyle's bedroom door closed, hoping she might be able to accomplish what she needed to without waking him up.

Based on the relaxed expression on his face, he'd be asleep for a while to come.

She grabbed a quick shower, slipped into a pair of jeans, a T-shirt and her jean jacket, and headed out. Nothing but silence filtered out of Kyle's bedroom.

Excellent.

She wanted to get out of the house and on her way without him being any the wiser.

She'd pulled the land coordinates next on the list and had marked them on a Denver area map in the middle of the night.

She was ready.

Sara pulled the front door shut behind her and hurried toward her car.

As she cranked on the ignition, she glanced down

at the markings on the map. If her calculations were correct, she should be able to reach her destination in just under an hour.

She had a fairly good sense of where she'd end up.

This particular parcel of property was one of the most beautiful in the region, privately owned by a local family for generations upon generations.

Sara only hoped she'd be able confirm ownership and warn all those connected to a possible sale before they ran out of time.

Fifty minutes later, she found herself on an unpaved access road that bordered the parcel. She eased her car to a stop along a stand of pines and climbed out, her boots sinking into the dusty road.

She'd been correct, ending up exactly where she'd imagined she would.

She planned to take a few pictures, document her findings, then locate the deed holder.

She reached back into the car for the digital camera she kept in the glove compartment then surveyed her surroundings. Breathtaking.

The lush land stretched as far as the eye could see and Sara smiled at the majestic mountains that swept skyward just off to the west above the tips of the evergreens spread before her.

She listened carefully, picking up the unmistakable sound of water running over the small falls she knew lay hidden inside this gem of a piece of land.

She lost herself for a moment, wondering what it

might be like to own such a piece of property, to have the power to protect it from development or drilling.

She thought of Annemarie momentarily and her heart twisted. For all her talk of social climbing, Annemarie had loved nothing more than the nature and beauty of the Colorado land and sky.

Maybe someday Sara would find a way to honor Annemarie's memory by making a difference in the things she'd loved.

Sara gave herself a mental shake and snapped her thoughts back into focus.

She could worry about "someday" another time.

Right now she had work to do.

She set off down the dirt road, staying clear of the foliage until she was farther along. She angled toward the trees then stopped to capture a shot of the expanse of land before her.

She made a notation in her small notebook, wanting a clear record of exactly where she'd been.

Sara wound her way through the pines, heading toward the sound of water.

The majestic surroundings and the crisp morning had cleared her head, sharpening her focus.

She'd make it through whatever ultimately happened between her and Kyle. She knew that now.

And she'd also wrap up this investigation.

She had no choice.

Sara knew she should turn back and head straight

for the PPS office to review her findings and plans, but she couldn't resist the pull of the running water and the sound of the falls.

As she stepped into a clearing, her breath caught.

Sunlight reflected off the clear stream, sparkling as it hit the rocks along the shore. She blew out a long sigh and was giving serious thought to climbing up a ways to sit and think, when she felt it.

A presence.

Someone was watching her.

Not something.

Someone.

She was sure of it.

A chill sliced through her and her scalp began to tingle. The meaning of both unmistakable.

Someone was out there. But who?

The landowner? Or the murderer?

Was it possible she'd been followed?

Sara fought the urge to look around, knowing the move would only serve to clue her pursuer to the fact she knew he was out there, even if she didn't know where.

She needed to continue as if she didn't suspect a thing. Sara swallowed down the anxiety clawing at her throat and reversed direction, doing her best to look relaxed and casual, when all she really wanted to do was to break into a sprint and run for her life.

She'd foolishly left both her cell phone and her gun in the glove compartment of her car, never con-

sidering she'd encounter danger at such a peaceful
location this early in the morning.

Fool.

She'd lost her investigative edge and she'd been
careless. If she'd been smart, she'd have run through
every possible scenario in her head before she began
this morning's operation.

Being followed or being discovered were definitely two scenarios she hadn't considered.

As the skin at the base of her neck began to crawl,
she cursed herself silently.

The new sensation meant only one thing.

Whoever was out there was moving closer.

And Sara had made a terrible mistake.

THE SIGHT of the empty pillow by his side hit Kyle
like a sucker punch. Not again.

A quick search of the house and a glance out front
proved his worst suspicion right. Sara's car was gone
and so was she.

But where?

He retraced his steps to her bedroom, breathing a
sigh of relief when he spotted the case folder still there.
So, wherever she'd gone, she hadn't needed their notes.

He raced for his office and plucked his cell phone
from his desk. He rang Sara, but frowned when his
call went immediately into voice mail.

He'd brought the folder of information with him
and now spread it methodically across his desktop.

He retraced their discussion from the night before, talking himself through the evidence piece by piece until he saw it.

The copy of the list of land coordinates from the mystery disk that had been sent to PPS was missing.

He should have known what Sara would do.

We have to force whoever is behind all of this out into the open. We have to let them know we're on to them.

Sara's words rattled through his brain.

Damn the woman.

She'd gone without him, making herself a target for whoever might be watching for their next move.

In her effort to save the life of the current owner, she may very well have put her own at risk. Kyle had to stop her, had to reach her before it was too late.

As much as it pained him, Kyle flipped open his cell and pulled Evangeline's number from his programmed list.

She answered immediately.

Kyle didn't waste any time on pleasantries. "Sara's vanished and I think she's gone off to check out the next set of land coordinates."

"Start at the beginning."

Although his stepmother's instruction irked the hell out of him, Kyle did as she asked, backing up to their lack of success at the office yesterday and to their success last night at downloading hard evidence against TCM.

He concluded with Sara's thought about chasing

down the next set of land coordinates on the list as the next investigative step.

"Give me the coordinates," Evangeline instructed, "and I'll have a team there immediately just in case."

"I can take care of this myself." Kyle tried to hide the defensive note in his voice, but failed miserably.

"Then why the call?"

He scowled at the superiority blatant in Evangeline's voice.

"I don't have the coordinates."

"But you've got everything there."

"Not anymore." He fanned the last set of sheets one more time. Nothing. "Apparently she doesn't want me following. She took them with her."

Silence beat across the line.

"Evangeline?" He waited. No response. "I don't ask you for much, but I'm asking you for this. I need those coordinates. If anything were to happen to her I'd—"

"Well, well," his stepmother interrupted. "It seems not only has your charm affected one of my best agents, but my agent seems to have affected your charm."

"The coordinates?"

Kyle scribbled down the digits as Evangeline read them off. Then he gratefully made note of the directions she provided.

She did, however, get in the final word before they disconnected the call.

"I *will* send backup, Kyle. Whether you think you can handle this or not."

Her implication rang loud and clear, but Kyle didn't waste time thinking about her harsh tone or her lack of confidence.

He was out the door and in his car in record time, coordinates and directions tucked into his shirt pocket.

Backup or no backup, he intended to find Sara before anyone else did.

As sharp as Sara was, she'd neglected to consider one very important thing.

Even though they'd overridden the printing system log last night at TCM, they hadn't overridden any other tracking device. And if whoever was behind this conspiracy was as brilliant as he seemed to be, then their mastermind already knew what Sara and Kyle had found, and he'd already anticipated their next step.

Kyle gunned the ignition and fishtailed the car out onto the road in a cloud of dust.

He could only hope he wasn't already too late.

COLD CHILLS had begun to race up and down Sara's spine.

She snagged the sleeve of her jacket on a pine tree, yelping slightly at the sudden impediment to her forward progress. Or was it backward progress?

As skilled as she was, and as carefully as she'd noticed her surroundings, sudden panic filled her that she might be going in circles with someone close on her heels.

She cleared a stand of pines, recognizing the lush foliage that ran along the river. The sound of waterfalls in the distance eased her fears a bit.

She'd been here before on her way onto the land parcel from her car.

She was all right.

She was headed in the right direction.

A sudden crashing behind her launched her out of her momentary celebration and into action.

She broke into a sprint, tree limbs clawing at her clothing, face and hair as she headed away from the noise and toward her car, weaving in and out of the trees to offer herself some small measure of camouflage.

Another noise.

Scuffling.

This time closer.

Much closer.

Damn.

Sara's heart pounded frantically and her pulse roared in her ears.

Calm. She had to stay calm.

If she could stay just far enough ahead of her pursuer to reach her car or her weapon—anything— she might have a chance.

Kyle's sleeping image flashed through her mind. She'd be damned if she wasn't going to be around to see that image again.

After she got out of this mess, she intended to lose

herself in the safe harbor of Kyle's arms. And she planned to tell him that he'd made her feel more alive than she'd felt since the night Annemarie died.

Sara clung to that image, clung to that hope, and quickened her pace. Running now, her breath grew short, a cramp seized her side.

She mentally blocked each sensation. Blocked each fear.

She moved forward, filled with one purpose only. Survival.

A shot rang out and she dropped to her knees, waiting a moment for a follow-up.

None came.

She hadn't been hit, so she scrambled on her hands and knees, pine needles scraping at her palms.

Why hadn't she awakened Kyle?

Why had she come alone?

What had she been thinking?

The bottom fell out of her stomach when she realized she hadn't even left Kyle a note and she'd taken the copy of the coordinates with her to keep him from following.

She'd have to rely on him to put the pieces together, to realize where she'd gone. To know she'd taken their next planned step without him.

She'd have to hope he'd reach out to PPS for help, for the coordinates in order to reach her in time.

Sara cleared the trees, scrambling onto the unpaved access road she'd used earlier.

She pushed to her feet and sprinted, hope flooding through her at the sight of her car, less than thirty yards ahead.

Another shot rang out and she dropped again, scrambling on her hands and knees.

She had to reach her car. Had to.

As if a mirage, the shape of another car approached in the distance. A small car. A sports car.

Kyle's car.

She was saved. He'd come for her. He'd come just in the nick of time.

Sara stood to wave him down, gesturing wildly while she ran a zigzag pattern to make herself a more difficult target.

But this time when she heard the crack of a rifle, searing pain exploded in her left shoulder.

The force of the gunshot sent her crashing to the packed dirt, needles and dust filling her mouth, her nose, her eyes as she hit the ground.

She reached for her arm, feeling the sticky blood as it seeped between her fingers.

And just as she heard Kyle's voice cry out, all sight and sound faded. Sara's world turned to black.

KYLE RACED his car down the access road, the tires slipping on the loose dirt and pine needles. He spotted a vehicle in the distance—Sara's—and pressed the accelerator to the floor, not caring that he sent a cloud of dust into the air behind him.

His gut screamed that something had gone horribly wrong, that Sara was in grave danger.

His instinct was proved correct when he pulled close enough to see past Sara's car, to see Sara herself, racing, running, gesturing wildly.

Kyle depressed the clutch and braked, launching himself from the car, even as he shoved the gearshift into Park and cut the engine.

He'd just cleared his car's hood when a shot cracked through the cool mountain air.

Kyle dropped instinctively, but kept his focus trained on Sara.

She went down. Hard. Her only motion was to reach for her shoulder.

"Sara!" Kyle pushed to his feet and broke into a full-out sprint, not thinking of the shooter out there somewhere, possibly still watching them, possibly getting away.

Kyle's only thought was of Sara, the woman he realized at that moment he didn't want to be without. He didn't want to grieve her loss, didn't want to ask himself "what if" for the rest of his life.

His only thought was of survival.

Sara's survival.

And he'd do whatever it took to ensure that reality.

He skidded to a stop by her side, sliding on his knees on the loose dirt. He cradled her head in his hands, calling to her, urging her back to consciousness.

She moaned, turning her head slightly toward his voice.

Kyle heard no other sound. Saw no other person or creature. The shooter must have fled.

"Sara. Sara." Kyle spoke her name gently, close to her ear. "Honey, do you hear me? You've got to wake up. Wake up. We're going to get you through this."

Her pale green eyes fluttered open. "Kyle."

"I'm right here."

"You've got to get him."

Even through her haze of pain and semiconsciousness she remained focused on the crime and not on her own mortality.

"He can wait." Kyle shrugged out of his jacket, rolled the material and used the crude pillow to elevate Sara's head. He next examined the site of her wound, gently probing until he could tell where the bullet had entered.

Sara cried out in pain and he winced. "Sorry, babe. Sorry."

"Don't call me *babe*," she ground out through gritted teeth. When their eyes met, he spotted the moisture shimmering in hers, but he also spotted the fire.

A flash of life and determination.

It was going to take more than a bullet to keep her down.

"You're going to be all right." He unbuttoned his shirt and stripped down to the T-shirt beneath.

He pressed his shirt to the wound, grimacing as

Sara moaned with the contact. "I think it missed your shoulder, but it's gone through your upper arm. I want you to hold this as tight as you can to slow the bleeding. I'll call for help."

Sara did as he asked and Kyle dashed for his car and the phone he'd left in the console. He dialed 911 and gave their location and situation. Much to his surprise a call had already been put in. From who?

The shooter?

Or from Evangeline?

She'd known where he'd been headed and she'd planned to send a team. Had she anticipated the worst?

Kyle raced back to Sara's side, dropping to his knees once more. "Help's already on its way."

Sara frowned slightly and Kyle pressed a kiss to her forehead. She closed her eyes then snapped them open, pinning him with a look more intense than he'd ever seen. "Go after him. Do not let him get away. We're close. So close. Please, Kyle."

Conflicting emotions tore at his insides. He wanted to stay and protect Sara. Wanted to hold her hand and keep pressure on her wound until help arrived.

Yet he also wanted to catch the bastard who had shot her. The bastard who had undoubtedly killed Jonathan Powers, Dwayne Johnson and the rest of the oil conspiracy victims.

"Go." The note of urgency in Sara's voice rang unmistakable. "I'll be all right. There's nothing more you can do for me here. Go."

Kyle pressed another kiss to her forehead and climbed to his feet.

"Through that far stand of trees." Her voice came with effort, her tone tight with pain. "Follow the river to the clearing, then cut into the forest. I first heard him there."

She grabbed for his leg as he moved to turn away. "Listen. Sense him. Trust your gut."

"I'll be right back," Kyle said as he turned to race after whoever had done this to Sara. "Stay put."

STAY PUT.

Even through her pain, those two words set Sara's teeth on edge. She knew it was her stupid pride talking, but it was something else, as well.

She was supposed to be out there protecting Kyle, not the other way around.

She struggled to a sitting position, pain slicing through her.

She couldn't let Kyle go out there alone, and she wasn't about to.

Sara grit her teeth and eased the balled-up shirt from her wound, wincing at the amount of blood that had saturated the material.

Kyle had said the wound seemed to be below her shoulder, through the upper arm itself. If that were the case, perhaps she could tie off the wound, or at least use Kyle's shirt as a wrap.

If her plan worked, she'd be able to slow the bleeding and give chase.

She had to follow Kyle, had to be there for him should he need her, should he need backup.

A sense of urgency overtook her senses, overrode the pain, and Sara set to work on the shirt, racing against time.

Rushing to reach Kyle before it was too late.

KYLE FOLLOWED the route Sara had described, stopping periodically to listen, hoping to hear some sound from Sara's attacker. A rustling. A scrambling through the foliage. Pine needles scattering along the forest floor. Something.

Instead he heard nothing.

He moved forward, following his gut once he reached the edge of the pines as Sara had said he would.

Kyle followed the edge of the stream, working to move quickly until he could reach the cover of the far trees.

Just as he reached the opposite edge of the open space, he heard them.

Footfalls.

Racing away from him.

Adrenaline spiked to life in his veins, and Kyle sprinted forward, injected with a renewed energy and determination.

He was going to catch Sara's shooter and he was

going to take that person down. He'd force a confession and he'd force information about everything else.

About the land deals.

About the forgeries.

About the murders.

Hope surged through him when he caught a flash of tan—a jacket sleeve exposed for a split second as the shooter worked through the maze of trees and shrubs.

The man seemed to slow and Kyle pushed himself to move faster, seizing the opportunity to close the space between them.

The openings between tree trunks increased and he could see the man's entire body ahead, still at quite a distance. Icy fingers gripped the back of Kyle's neck and he swallowed, slowing momentarily as he recognized the height and build.

Recognized the perfectly groomed hair, the dark blond color, the flawless cut.

And as the shooter stopped and turned, slowly revealing himself, Kyle staggered, momentarily losing his footing as he stared into the familiar face. The familiar eyes.

Emerald eyes.

Evil eyes.

Peter.

Chapter Fifteen

"Fancy meeting you here." Peter smirked at Kyle as he spoke the words. "And just when I was having so much fun."

"You bastard." Kyle launched himself at his half brother, momentarily forgetting all about his gun.

When Peter raised a pistol, training it on Kyle's face, Kyle had no choice but to grind to a halt. He swallowed and his insides tilted sideways.

What had he been thinking?

He'd seen Peter and he'd lost all rational thought.

He tipped his chin toward the gun. "You're not going to tell me that's what you shot her with, are you?"

Peter pursed his lips and grinned. "No. This little beauty's just for backup. I ditched my rifle a ways back." One eyebrow crooked. "I can see you still possess those sound tracking skills you always had as a kid."

Kyle narrowed his gaze, wishing he could some-how have Peter in hand-to-hand battle, like two men, without the gun. He'd take him down, no doubt about it. He just had to figure out a way how.

"Why did you shoot her?" Kyle asked, all the while working possible scenarios for escape and Peter's capture through his head.

Peter shrugged. "Why not? She wasn't receptive at all to my charms, so I really had no use for her. When I realized she was working with you to expose all of my hard work, she had to go."

"What's one more body, right?"

Kyle was fishing with his question, but Peter's response momentarily stunned him just the same.

"That's funny. That's exactly what I was thinking when I pulled the trigger."

"How many, Peter?"

His half brother gave another shrug, this one more exaggerated. "How many what?"

"How many investors? How many landowners? How many innocent people have you killed?"

Peter leveled a glare at him, all trace of warmth gone from his vivid eyes. "Why, Kyle, I don't know what you're talking about."

"And the signatures. How did you forge my signature?" Kyle risked a step closer. When Peter didn't respond he took two more.

Peter waved the gun at Kyle's head. "You know, if you used any of those brains you've put to waste, you'd know how simple it is to forge anything electronic with the right access key."

Kyle nodded. "My mistake." So he'd been correct about the process, he'd just been way off the mark in terms of the culprit's identity.

He frowned. "What about Johnson?"

"Stupid." Peter thinned his lips. "He honestly thought he'd get away with stealing company documents. Can you imagine? As if I'd let a loose cannon like him walk around unchecked."

"He believed your handiwork, believed I was behind everything."

Peter tipped his head from side to side. "I'm very good at what I do. Quite skilled, actually."

Kyle moved yet closer while his brother bragged, his heart now pounding rapid and steady against his ribs. If he could only get close enough while Peter wasn't paying full attention, he might be able to knock the gun from his hands.

"If you think I'm unaware of you closing in on me, big brother, think again." Peter waved the gun. "Actually, you're doing me a favor. When I shoot you and leave you for dead, I want to make sure I don't miss."

"Like you did with Sara?"

Kyle took satisfaction in the angry flash of emotion that crossed Peter's face.

"I did not miss her," he snarled.

"No?" Kyle stepped closer still. "Then why is she back at her car now, briefing the first responders on exactly what happened?" He pointed to his own arm. "Flesh wound, Peter. You must be losing your touch."

"That was no flesh wound."

Kyle shrugged, mimicking Peter's earlier gesture. "You think what you want."

"What I want is to see you dead." Now it was Peter who took a step closer. "I've wanted to see you dead for as long as I can remember."

Kyle steeled himself, unwilling to show the slightest reaction to the cold hatred seething from his brother's eyes.

He knew Peter spoke the truth. Peter had never done anything to hide his contempt for Kyle. Their fights as children had been legendary.

But Kyle had typically outmuscled his smaller brother, and his muscles itched to do that very thing right now.

Peter had gone silent, his features focused and intent. He steadied the pistol and took aim, his finger moving on the trigger.

Kyle had to keep him talking.

"What about running me off the road? You?"

Peter nodded. "Yes. I loved seeing your bike go over the edge as I drove away. Too bad you survived, as you always do." The gun faltered slightly. "It's as though you have a protective shield. Too bad that's all going to change."

"What about Buddy Forman? On your payroll?"

Again Peter nodded. "The beauty of the man is that he'll do whatever he's told. For a price."

"Powers?"

"I had Buddy take him out after I set up a phony meeting by saying I was you. Buddy waited for him, then stashed the body until you and your girlfriend had stopped searching."

"How'd you manage the gun? The fingerprints?"

Peter laughed, the sound starting deep and growing louder and louder. A chill slid down Kyle's spine.

His brother was insane.

"It's called ingenuity," Peter said, once again waving the gun. "It's not that difficult to lift prints from one thing and transfer them to another, and stealing your gun was child's play. I just waited until you were off on one of your infamous bike rides."

"Why did you show up here today?"

Peter retrained the pistol on Kyle, his finger once again inching toward the trigger.

"I know everything that goes on at TCM, including every file that's accessed or downloaded. I'm not stupid."

"No." Kyle shook his head. "No one ever accused you of that."

"Don't move or I'll shoot."

Sara's voice rang out loud and strong through the still air. Kyle moved to turn to see her, but Peter shook his head.

"You move, I'll shoot," he said. "It's that simple."

"You'll be dead before you can pull the trigger," Sara answered.

Kyle knew she was bluffing. He'd seen the extent

of her wound, and he'd seen her very obvious pain. The stubborn woman had followed him instead of waiting for help.

The prospect of Peter killing him was one thing, but the prospect of Peter killing Sara was something Kyle couldn't bear to think about.

"Sara." He tipped his head slightly to call out over his shoulder, his arms held out, palms front. "Go back and wait for help. Don't be stupid. There's no telling what he'll do."

"Sure there is." Her response was sharp and quick. "He'll shoot you and then he'll die, downed by just one bullet from my gun. I'm that good."

Kyle watched the smile of amusement that spread across Peter's face. He was enjoying the entire process.

"She's something, isn't she?" Peter said.

Kyle could see Sara moving in his peripheral vision. She was closing in, yet moving to Peter's side at the same time, no doubt trying to pull his aim from Kyle.

Unfortunately, the move didn't seem to be having the slightest effect on Peter's focus.

"You know—" Peter's brows snapped together "—I seem to remember your sister, Annemarie, putting on a show of bravado herself." He paused dramatically, then smiled. "Right before I killed her."

Sara gasped and Kyle felt her shock and pain.

She staggered, and for a split second Peter flinched, no doubt taken by the effect of his own words.

Kyle didn't take time to think. He merely reacted.

He made his move in one swift and sure motion, lunging for Peter's waist, just below the level of the gun.

When he connected his shoulder to Peter's ribs, he heard a satisfying pop and saw the gun fly out of Peter's hand.

The two men hit the dirt and pine needles in a tangle of arms and legs, rolling as they each fought to overpower the other.

Peter swung and connected, sending a burst of pain through Kyle's jaw. Kyle scrambled, planting his feet and standing, lunging toward Peter once again and taking him down, this time smiling at the sharp outburst of air from Peter as the wind was knocked from his lungs.

Peter struggled to free himself, struggled to get the other hand, but Kyle was bigger and stronger. He maneuvered to lock his arm around his brother's neck, feeling nothing but stunned when Peter took an evasive move and Kyle lost his grip.

He couldn't afford to blow this. Couldn't afford to lose.

The only hope for getting both him and Sara out of this forest alive was for Kyle to fight Peter until the bitter end.

And he planned to do just that.

SARA STAGGERED with the force of Peter's harsh words.

He'd killed Annemarie. But how? He'd been no more than a little boy. It wasn't possible, was it?

She jerked her thoughts out of the past and into the present as she watched Kyle careen into Peter and slam him to the ground.

Something flashed as it hit the dirt and Sara realized Peter's weapon had been ripped from his grip.

As Kyle and Peter rolled away from the point of impact, Sara scrambled to where Peter had stood, trying to ignore the increasing pain and weakness in her arm.

She spotted the gun and picked it up, flipping on its safety and tucking it into the back of her jeans.

All she had to do now was wait for her opportunity to break up the fight, to shoot Peter if necessary, to save Kyle from the sure death his brother had planned.

But the two men were indistinguishable from one another as they struggled and rolled, dirt and dust and fists flying.

She raised her weapon and aimed, hoping for a clear shot of Peter's tan jacket, but she was unable to get a shot that wouldn't risk injuring Kyle's bare arm or back or head.

The two brothers grunted and groaned, swearing loudly at each other, years of hate and anger pouring out of their systems.

When the *thump-thump-thump* of a helicopter sounded overhead, growing nearer, Sara's hope soared.

Suddenly a voice sounded from a loudspeaker. "Denver police. We have you surrounded. Get down on the ground with your hands behind your heads."

Sara rolled her eyes. Neither man responded, nor were they going to. Even if the booming voice had found a way inside their narrow field of concentration, neither one was going to go down a loser.

That's when she realized what she had to do.

Sara pointed her gun and fired into the ground where she knew her shot couldn't injure Kyle or Peter, or ricochet and clip some well-hidden member of the Denver police.

The sudden crack had its intended effect.

Kyle and Peter pushed away from each other, both scrambling to their feet. But while Kyle repositioned himself, fists at the ready, Peter reached into his boot.

And pulled out yet another weapon.

In the blink of an eye, he brought up his hand, gun leveled at Kyle's face.

As Sara screamed out a warning, a single gunshot sounded.

Her heart seized in her chest as she waited for Kyle to fall. Tears blurred her vision, but then the unthinkable happened.

Peter staggered, then buckled, dropping to the forest floor in a heap.

Kyle kicked the gun clear of his hand, then lifted his gaze to Sara's. "Are you all right?" he asked.

She nodded, not trying to fight the sting of tears that spilled over her lower lashes. "You?"

He smiled at her, moving to pull her into his arms. "Never better."

Peter moaned and rolled over. Kyle pulled Sara to his side as they stood over the man who had wanted them both dead.

Thrashing sounds in the foliage behind them told them help was closing in fast.

The shot that had taken Peter down must have come from a sharpshooter, and from quite a distance.

"Why?" Kyle spoke the word with such emotion, Sara's heart ached.

"Because you had everything," Peter ground out through gritted teeth.

"Everything?" Kyle shook his head incredulously. "I had a mother who cared more about your father and money than she cared about anything else. I had a father who never tried to know me until it was too late."

"None of that matters," Peter hissed.

Kyle couldn't believe what he was hearing. Was his half brother mad?

"People like you." Peter's voice went flat, growing weak. "They never liked me."

Could this entire nightmare go back to something rooted so far back in their childhood? Was it possible?

"You orchestrated this conspiracy and put my name to it because you were jealous?" Kyle barely recognized his own voice, his tone had gone so tight with disbelief.

Peter gave the slightest shake of his head. "I'm not the mastermind, but using your name was my idea. A stroke of real genius. The icing on a perfect cake."

"But you didn't get away with it."

"I would have." The color had begun to rapidly drain from Peter's face. "I would have."

Kyle looked at Sara. "Where are they?"

"I hear them. They're coming." She nodded, her eyes huge.

"You." Peter managed a weak laugh, shifting his gaze to Sara. "I should have killed you just like I killed your sister."

Kyle reached for Sara's hand, but she'd taken a step back out of his reach.

"I told her I lost my kitten and she believed me. I'd always wondered what it would be like to kill someone."

He coughed, gasping for air. "Wondered what it would be like to snuff out a light so bright."

Fury surged through Kyle at the expression of sheer bliss on Peter's face. Even through his pain, the memory of taking Annemarie Montgomery's life brought a smile to the man's lips.

Brother or no brother, a monster like Peter Turner deserved to live only so that he could be punished for his crimes.

"How could you—" Sara's voice trailed away at the end of her question.

"Baseball bat," Peter answered. "I was always a strong kid."

"Damn you." Kyle dropped to his knees and gripped Peter's shirt, shaking him just as their rescuers' footsteps grew near. "And the landowners and investors? Why?"

"You'll never know how deep this goes." Peter leered.

Kyle could barely make out Peter's words, his voice had grown so weak.

"It's over now," Kyle said. "It ends today."

Peter's lips twisted into a smirk. "Not over. Even if I die. Not over."

Peter's features grew slack and Kyle felt for a pulse. Present, but weak.

"He's lost consciousness," he said flatly.

As the police and emergency workers arrived, Kyle stepped back, taking Sara's hand and pulling her aside for a moment before they worked on her wound.

"He'll never hurt anyone again," Kyle said.

Tears swam in Sara's eyes, but she blinked, trying to clear them.

Kyle rubbed his thumb across her cheek. "Come here."

He pulled her gently into his arms, and she relaxed against him. Kyle held her, realizing he never wanted to let go, sheltering her in his arms until the paramedics moved to treat her wound.

As Kyle gave his detailed statement to the same two detectives who had taken him in on suspicion of Powers's murder just two days earlier, the only thing he was conscious of—fully conscious of—was Peter's statement.

You'll never know how deep this goes.

If Peter wasn't the mastermind, then whoever had been pulling the strings—and getting rich—was still out there. Somewhere. And Kyle was determined to do whatever it took to find that person and take him down.

But he wanted Sara out of the investigation. He wanted her safe and sheltered, recovering somewhere quiet where no one could touch her.

He knew Sara would put up an argument, but Kyle didn't care.

He had no intention of coming this close to losing her ever again. She might as well start getting used to his protectiveness.

Kyle planned to practice the skill for the rest of his life.

Evangeline no doubt had other capable agents at PPS who could see the investigation through to its conclusion.

Kyle would do whatever they wanted. He'd cooperate with whatever they needed.

He would not rest until the force behind the land and oil conspiracy was taken down, once and for all.

Chapter Sixteen

Kyle approached the guarded door of Peter's hospital room and stopped at the sight inside.

His stepfather stood vigil next to Peter's bed, although Stephen's expression looked anything but sympathetic.

When Kyle tapped against the door frame, Stephen lifted his focus, giving a weak smile when he spotted Kyle.

"Bad time?" Kyle asked.

Stephen gave a slight shake of his head. "I'm surprised to see you here. After what he did."

"Yes, well, he's still my flesh and blood."

"As hard as that may be for us to believe." Stephen's tone was heavy with a dejection Kyle had never heard before. "I always knew he had a dark side, but I never imagined…"

"None of us did." Kyle pressed his palm to his stepfather's shoulder as the other man's words trailed off. "Any sign of him coming out of the coma?"

Stephen breathed in deeply. "Hard to say. The doctor tells me it could be hours or it could be months, or longer."

"He was ready to kill me." Kyle spoke the words flatly, knowing they'd only add to Stephen's heartache, but needing to voice them. "He was ready to shoot me and leave me for dead out in the forest."

"I'm sorry."

Kyle thinned his lips, scrutinizing the almost lifeless figure of his half brother. "It's not your fault."

"I must have failed him somewhere." Stephen turned, leveling a tired look at Kyle. "Just as I failed you."

Kyle raked a hand through his hair. "You never failed me."

"But I could have been there for you more." Stephen looked back at Peter. "You weren't like him. He was needy. You weren't."

"Thanks, I think."

Stephen scrubbed a hand across his face and Kyle noticed deep lines of fatigue. The man's jaw also sported at least a day's worth of stubble.

The mighty Stephen Turner's appearance was a far cry from that of the polished CEO Kyle had known most of his life.

"I need to stretch my legs." Stephen stepped toward Kyle and led him out into the hall. "He confessed to everything?"

Kyle nodded, almost sorry to be the one to confirm how evil Stephen's own son had become. "Everything except masterminding the conspiracy. That demon's still out there somewhere.

"They've found evidence at his home linking him to each of the murders. He kept photos of each victim as souvenirs."

Stephen winced then searched Kyle's face. "He was jealous of you, you know. But I never dreamed he'd do anything like this to hurt you."

"I still don't understand it." Kyle worked to calm his growing frustration. "Why the hell would he be jealous of me?"

Stephen splayed a palm on Kyle's shoulder and Kyle found the uncommon gesture oddly comforting. "You say what you mean and you mean what you say. You may not have the best work ethic in the world, but you've got a good heart. People see that. And your brother was jealous."

"I'm going to change the work-ethic thing." Kyle did his best to keep a defensive tone out of his voice.

"I think you already have."

They stood in companionable silence for a few moments, then Stephen patted Kyle's shoulder and turned back toward Peter's room.

He hesitated at the door, looking back.

"I'm sorry I never paid enough attention to you, Kyle. That's going to change. It's just that I sensed you didn't need me."

"You sensed wrong." Kyle spoke the words surely, from his heart.

Stephen jerked his thumb toward Peter's bed. "I want to be here when he wakes up and wants to atone for his sins."

"Good luck with that," Kyle said as he turned to walk away.

He was quite sure Peter had zero intention of atoning for his sins, no matter what happened. No matter what plea agreement he might make in order to bring the conspiracy's mastermind to justice.

His half brother was evil.

Kyle had heard it in his voice and seen it in his eyes.

Peter had tried to kill Sara, and he'd intended to kill Kyle.

He would have.

If Sara Montgomery hadn't saved Kyle's life by firing off a shot and breaking Peter's focus.

What a difference a week made. Before Sara walked into his stepfather's party, Kyle had convinced himself he liked his playboy reputation, but now he'd seen the light. The light in Sara's eyes that said she believed in him. Something Kyle hadn't seen in anyone's eyes since his father's death.

He was determined to turn his life around, determined to make a difference at TCM or somewhere else. Maybe he'd do what Sara had suggested. Perhaps he'd put his money where his mouth was and start a land preservation foundation.

The future was wide open, but there was just one item he had to take care of first.

And one person he had to see.

SARA SAT OUTSIDE her parents' house and thought about how long it had been since she'd last set foot inside. It had been years since she'd shared a meal with the two people who had given her life, even if her life hadn't turned out the way they'd wanted.

How many Mother's Days and Father's Days had she missed?

Well—she pushed open the driver's door and stepped out into the beautiful June day—enough was enough.

The drive from Denver to Aurora had taken her only a half hour, but she'd done a lot of thinking.

Knowing that Kyle planned to make a tentative effort to forge a relationship with Stephen Turner had inspired her.

If those two could move beyond the past, surely Sara and her parents could do the same.

It was time to overcome the obstacle that had stood between them for so long.

The mystery of Annemarie's death.

Sara stepped onto the front step and froze, finger poised to press the doorbell.

She wasn't sure how long she'd been standing there when the front door opened. Her mother's serious features measured her carefully.

"I thought you might never push that button," her mother said, the lines around her hazel eyes softening with her smile. "Welcome home, honey."

Her mother held her arms wide and Sara hesitated for only a second, moving into her mother's embrace and wrapping her own arms around the waist of the woman she'd missed so much. Sara hadn't realized how much until this very moment.

Still recovering from her gunshot wound, she winced as her mother squeezed her.

"You all right?" her mother asked.

Sara nodded. "Perfect." She wasn't about to mention getting shot on her first visit home.

"Who's there, Maggie?" her father called out.

Sara stiffened and her mother clucked her tongue in her ear. "Don't you dare pull away from me. I've waited a long time for this."

Sara tucked her face into her mother's neck. "I'm sorry, Mom."

"We're sorry too, honey. So sorry."

Her father's sharp intake of air was audible when he reached the front door.

"Well, I'll be—"

This time when Sara straightened, her mother eased her grip enough to let Sara look at her father.

"Hi, Dad."

He patted Sara's cheek as he'd done so many times in a past that seemed so long ago. Sara's vision swam. Years of pent-up emotion strangled her and she searched for the right words to tell her parents why she'd come home after all this time.

"I finally know what happened."

Pain crossed both of her parents' faces.

Silence filled the space surrounding them for several seconds.

"Her death wasn't your fault." Her mother's throat worked. "We were wrong to let you carry that guilt. You were just a kid."

"It wasn't your fault," her dad repeated.

For the first time in fifteen years, a weight began to lift from Sara's shoulders and a chip began to fall away.

Annemarie's death wasn't her fault.

It had never been her fault.

It had been the fault of a sick, twisted little boy who had wanted to know what it would feel like to kill someone.

Sara's mother stepped back and held out her hands. "Come in, honey."

They shared a meal and caught up on the years they'd wasted. Sara told her parents all about her work with the FBI and with PPS. She also told them every word of Peter Turner's confession.

The three of them shed fresh tears, but Sara knew in her heart that their healing had finally begun.

Before she headed back to Denver, she climbed the familiar stairs to the second floor, wanting to see the rooms where she and Annemarie had grown up.

Both bedrooms stood untouched, as if the young

women who had once lived there would be back at any moment to resume the lives that had been shattered by a killer.

Sara leaned against the doorjamb to her old bedroom and took a visual inventory, her jaw slack with disbelief.

Not a thing had been changed. Every memento, poster and knickknack was just how she'd left it all those years ago.

Her parents had made her room a memorial as if she'd been lost to them just as Annemarie had been.

Sara hung her head in shame.

She had been lost to them—thoroughly lost.

She remembered her parting words clearly. How she'd told them she hoped she'd never see them again.

How could they ever forgive her?

The weight of her mother's arm anchored around her waist.

"I was so wrong to leave like I did."

Her mother gave her a quick shake. "Nonsense. You're here now, aren't you?"

Sara nodded, too overcome by emotion to speak.

"Now then, if you'll promise to visit regularly, I can finally box all of this up and give your father the office he's always wanted."

"I promise." A bubble of warmth burst deep inside Sara and spread through her, starting at her very core and reaching outward.

"What about Annemarie's room?"

She turned to study her mother's reaction, surprised to see her smile never wavered.

"I always did want to take up sewing."

They shared a long, knowing look and then linked hands, turning away from the past.

Sara headed back to Denver with the promise to come back for Sunday dinner.

Maybe she'd bring Kyle—if he'd agree to come.

Nerves fluttered in her stomach at the thought of asking him and she laughed out loud.

Here she sat, a model FBI agent turned investigator and the thought of asking a man—a younger man, at that—to dinner at her parents' house unnerved her.

Well, no one had ever called Sara Montgomery a coward, and she'd be darned sure they weren't going to start now.

SHE FOUND KYLE up at the lookout where they'd first kissed. She'd waited for him at his house, but when he hadn't returned home from the hospital, she'd known just where to find him.

And she'd been right.

The sun had begun to slide behind the mountain peaks, casting a lavender glow over the mounds of rock and valleys of earth.

She'd never seen anything more beautiful.

Kyle heard her approach and turned to meet her, a genuine smile spreading wide across his face.

"I was just thinking about you," he said.

"No kidding?" Sara slipped her arm around his waist and moved close to his side as he pulled her against him.

"It's true," he answered. "I was wondering if you'd like to give up law enforcement to help me save all this."

Would she? Could she?

She wasn't sure.

"How much time do I have to give you my answer?"

Kyle reached into his pocket and pulled out a small velvet box. "I was planning on giving you the rest of your life, but that depends on your answer to my second question."

Sara swallowed down the sudden lump in her throat, unable to believe her eyes. Kyle opened the box and the most exquisite diamond solitaire Sara had ever seen glimmered inside.

Kyle dropped his arm from her shoulders and kneeled in front of her, looking up at her, smile lines creasing the skin on either side of his beautiful eyes.

"Sara Montgomery." His grin pulled crooked and Sara's heart swelled. "Will you marry me?"

She pressed her lips together, fighting the urge to pinch herself.

"Are you sure?" Her voice climbed an octave.

"Of course I'm sure." Kyle's brows snapped together. "What kind of question is that?"

Sara laughed then—a sudden, carefree burst of air. She nodded.

Kyle cupped a hand to his ear. "What's that? I couldn't quite hear you."

"Yes." She held out her hand to pull Kyle to his feet.

When they stood toe-to-toe, her gaze locked with his, she gave her answer a second time.

"Yes."

He closed his mouth over hers and Sara let herself melt into the arms of the man she loved with all her heart.

When he broke away, he turned them both so they once more faced the fading sun.

"It's a magical place," he said.

"Yes, it is."

They stood in companionable silence for a few moments, but then Sara remembered he'd been to see Stephen and the investigator in her took over. "How was it?"

"Good." Kyle nodded his head. "Peter's still in his coma, but I think Stephen and I will be all right. In time. You?"

She grinned, feeling warm all over again at the memory of her trip home. "It was wonderful."

"They were glad to see you?"

She nodded.

"I hate to say I told you so, but—"

"You told me so," she interrupted.

Kyle held up one finger then headed toward his car. "Don't move."

Sara watched as he reached into the backseat and

worked on something for several long moments. When he emerged, he held two glasses of champagne.

He handed one to Sara as he stood once more, facing her.

"We just need one more thing."

He lowered his own glass then pulled the velvet box from his pocket one more time. This time when he opened the lid, he pulled the sparkling ring free of the case.

"Wow."

"Wow is right." He grinned as he took Sara's hand and slid the ring onto her finger. "Perfect. I hope you like it."

"I love it."

The mood turned suddenly serious as soon as she spoke the words. Kyle's features fell slack and he searched her face.

"I love you, Sara. I've loved you since you first faked your way into my life."

She bit down on her lip and smiled. "And I've loved you since you first called me *babe*."

His gaze narrowed. "I always knew you secretly liked that."

"Right."

Kyle hoisted his glass and Sara did the same.

"To new beginnings," he toasted. "And to a long, boring life filled with nothing but love and happiness."

They clinked their glasses and toasted their futures.

Then, as the last sliver of sun faded out of sight, they sealed the deal. Kissing one last time up on the lookout before they headed home.

Together.

Epilogue

When Angel appeared at Evangeline's door looking even paler than usual, Evangeline instantly sensed that something had gone horribly wrong.

Only, the words that came out of Angel's mouth delivered the opposite news.

Something had gone unbelievably right.

"Robert's on the line for you." Angel spoke slowly, as if she couldn't believe what she was saying.

"Robert who?" Evangeline asked, but her heart had quickened its beating.

It couldn't be *her* Robert. It couldn't be. He was dead.

"Robert," Angel said, her meaning clear.

Evangeline worked to keep her voice under control and gave a dismissive wave of her hand. "Close the door."

She reached for the phone, watching the blinking light indicate the line on hold. She steadied herself and took a deep breath.

When she answered the line, she said nothing, not trusting her voice. Not wanting to let the hope she'd held inside for so long spread through her if this was all a cruel joke.

"I've missed you."

And with just those three words, spoken in the voice of the man she'd loved so fiercely and missed so deeply, her world began to right itself.

"Me, too," she said. "Where are you?"

"I'm ready to come back."

"Why now?"

"It's time to get my revenge."

"Against who?" Evangeline's mind whirled with the surreal quality of the call and their conversation.

"You dispatch the agents I know you're about to dispatch and I'll be in touch."

"But, Robert—"

"No names. Not yet." He said nothing for a moment. "I'll see you soon."

The line clicked dead in Evangeline's ear and she sat at her desk, stunned.

She had to gather herself, had to tell the staff that had grieved their leader for so long and so intensely that he'd survived. He'd survived and was ready to seek his revenge.

But against who? And why?

I'll see you soon.

Evangeline took a deep breath as she pushed away from her desk and stepped toward her office door.

The staff had already assembled, obviously alerted by Angel to the call and the caller's identity.

"So I see you've all heard."

Heads nodded and voices murmured words of shock and surprise. Every pair of eyes remained riveted to Evangeline's face, bright with expectation and amazement.

"It's true." She delivered the news standing up, remaining steady without leaning on a desk, a wall, anything. "Robert is very much alive. And ready to seek his revenge."

Every set of eyes in the room squinted, measuring her actions, measuring her words.

She knew these people well enough to know exactly what they were thinking.

They were wondering why she hadn't screamed in joy, or fainted with shock.

But Evangeline fought to keep her face expressionless.

So Robert was alive.

She had thought she'd feel a sense of shock and surprise at the news. She'd imagined the moment. Many times. The reality was she'd never fully believed the reports of her husband's death.

He was too smart, too clever, to have died as witnesses had claimed.

There was another component to her suspicions, as well.

She'd never lost their connection, never lost that

piece of her that felt alive as long as Robert was near. Surely that part of her soul, that corner of her heart, would have died the moment he died.

But it hadn't.

And somewhere deep inside she'd always suspected—and hoped—this day would come.

I'll see you soon.

Evangeline shoved the myriad thoughts out of her mind, focusing on what needed to be done, just as Robert had said.

She needed to act on the information Sara Montgomery had presented before she'd left on a well-deserved recuperative getaway with Kyle.

While none of the paperwork they'd found had listed any investor names, one agreement of sale had listed an offshore account—and that account's location.

Evangeline tipped her head toward Lily Clark and John Pinto.

She ignored the stares of the rest of the agents, who undoubtedly couldn't believe her cold enough to conduct business when she'd just learned her dead husband wasn't dead at all.

"You two. Start packing. You'll be on the next charter to Cuerva. And make sure you stop by tech support on your way out.

"I want to be sure you have every bit of technology necessary to crack open those offshore accounts.

"Let's bring this mess to a close, once and for all."

* * * * *

*Don't miss John Pinto and Lily Clark's most
important assignment as*
***BODYGUARDS UNLIMITED,
DENVER, COLORADO***
*continues next month.
Look for*
NAVAJO ECHOES
*by Cassie Miles,
only from Harlequin Intrigue!*

THE ROYAL HOUSE OF NIROLI
Always passionate, always proud

The richest royal family in the world—united by
blood and passion, torn apart by deceit and desire

Nestled in the azure blue of the Mediterranean Sea, the
majestic island of Niroli has prospered for centuries.
The Fierezza men have worn the crown with passion
and pride since ancient times. But now, as the king's
health declines, and his two sons have been tragically
killed, the crown is in jeopardy.

The clock is ticking—a new heir must be found
before the king is forced to abdicate. By royal decree
the internationally scattered members of the Fierezza
family are summoned to claim their destiny. But any
person who takes the throne must do so according to
The Rules of the Royal House of Niroli. Soon secrets
and rivalries emerge as the descendents of this ancient
royal line vie for position and power. Only a true
Fierezza can become ruler—a person dedicated to their
country, their people…and their eternal love!

Each month starting in July 2007,
Harlequin Presents is delighted to bring you
an exciting installment from
THE ROYAL HOUSE OF NIROLI,
in which you can follow the epic search
for the true Nirolian king.
Eight heirs, eight romances, eight fantastic stories!

Here's your chance to enjoy a sneak preview of the
first book delivered to you by royal decree…

FIVE minutes later she was standing immobile in front of the study's window, her original purpose of coming in forgotten, as she stared in shocked horror at the envelope she was holding. Waves of heat followed by icy chill surged through her body. She could hardly see the address now through her blurred vision, but the crest on its left-hand front corner stood out, its *royal* crest, followed by the address: *HRH Prince Marco of Niroli…*

She didn't hear Marco's key in the apartment door, she didn't even hear him calling out her name. Her shock was so great that nothing could penetrate it. It encased her in a kind of bubble, which only concentrated the torment of what she was suffering and branded it on her brain so that it could never be forgotten. It was only finally pierced by the sudden opening of the study door as Marco walked in.

"Welcome home, *Your Highness*. I suppose I ought to curtsy." She waited, praying that he would laugh and tell her that she had got it all wrong, that the envelope she was holding, addressing him as Prince Marco of Niroli, was some silly mistake. But like a tiny candle flame shivering vulnerably in the dark, her hope trembled fearfully. And then the look in Marco's eyes extinguished it as cruelly as a hand placed callously over a dying person's face to stem their last breath.

"Give that to me," he demanded, taking the envelope from her.

"It's too late, Marco," Emily told him brokenly. "I know the truth now…." She dug her teeth in her lower lip to try to force back her own pain.

"You had no right to go through my desk," Marco shot back at her furiously, full of loathing at being caught off-guard and forced into a position in which he was in the wrong, making him determined to find something he could accuse Emily of. "I trusted you…."

Emily could hardly believe what she was hearing. "No, you didn't trust me, Marco, and you didn't trust me because you knew that I couldn't trust you. And you knew that because you're a liar, and liars don't trust people because they know that they themselves cannot be trusted." She not only felt sick, she also felt as though she could hardly breathe. "You are Prince Marco of Niroli…. How could you not tell me who you are and still live with me as intimately as we have lived together?" she demanded brokenly.

"Stop being so ridiculously dramatic," Marco

demanded fiercely. "You are making too much of the situation."

"Too much?" Emily almost screamed the words at him. "When were you going to tell me, Marco? Perhaps you just planned to walk away without telling me anything? After all, what do my feelings matter to you?"

"Of course they matter." Marco stopped her sharply. "And it was in part to protect them, and you, that I decided not to inform you when my grandfather first announced that he intended to step down from the throne and hand it on to me."

"To protect me?" Emily nearly choked on her fury. "Hand on the throne? No wonder you told me when you first took me to bed that all you wanted was sex. You *knew* that was the only kind of relationship there could ever be between us! You *knew* that one day you would be Niroli's king. No doubt you are expected to marry a princess. Is she picked out for you already, your *royal* bride?"

* * * * *

Look for
THE FUTURE KING'S PREGNANT MISTRESS
by Penny Jordan in July 2007,
from Harlequin Presents,
available wherever books are sold.

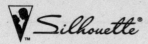

Silhouette®

Romantic
SUSPENSE

**Sparked by Danger,
Fueled by Passion.**

Mission: Impassioned

A brand-new miniseries begins with

My Spy

By *USA TODAY* bestselling author

Marie Ferrarella

She had to trust him with her life....
It was the most daring mission of Joshua Lazlo's
career: rescuing the prime minister of England's
daughter from a gang of cold-blooded kidnappers.
But nothing prepared the shadowy secret agent
for a fiery woman whose touch ignited something
far more dangerous.

My Spy

#1472

Available July 2007 wherever you buy books!

Do you know a real-life heroine?

Nominate her for the Harlequin More Than Words award.

Each year Harlequin Enterprises honors five ordinary women for their extraordinary commitment to their community.

Each recipient of the Harlequin More Than Words award receives a $10,000 donation from Harlequin to advance the work of her chosen charity. And five of Harlequin's most acclaimed authors donate their time and creative talents to writing a novella inspired by the award recipients. The More Than Words anthology is published annually in October and all proceeds benefit causes of concern to women.

HARLEQUIN

More Than Words™

**For more details or to nominate
a woman you know please visit**

www.HarlequinMoreThanWords.com

MTW2007

nocturne™

**DON'T MISS THE RIVETING CONCLUSION
TO THE RAINTREE TRILOGY**

RAINTREE: SANCTUARY

by *New York Times* bestselling author

BEVERLY
BARTON

Mercy, guardian of the Raintree
homeplace, takes a stand against
the Ansara wizards to battle for
the Clan's future.

*On sale July,
wherever books are sold.*